Unfinished business...

"I don't think there's any point in rehashing something that was—that was never anything more than—a mild aberration, on both our parts," she declared, hoping she sounded more convincing than she felt. "I—was going through a bad time, and you were there. I was—grateful. But that's all there was to it."

Ben crossed the space between them, and clamped his hands to her shoulders. "Don't bait me, Jaime," he added, his hard fingers pressing against the fine material of her dress. "You might have been able to fool that crazy brother of mine, but I know you. Better than he ever did, I'd say."

ANNE MATHER began her career by writing the kind of book she likes to read—romance. Married, with two children, this author from the north of England has become a favorite with readers of romance fiction the world over—her books have been translated into many languages and are read in countless countries. Since her first novel was published in 1970, Anne Mather has written more than eighty romances, with over ninety million copies sold!

Books by Anne Mather

STORMSPELL
WILD CONCERTO
HIDDEN IN THE FLAME
THE LONGEST PLEASURE

HARLEQUIN PRESENTS
1354—INDISCRETION
1444—BLIND PASSION
1458—SUCH SWEET POISON
1492—BETRAYED
1514—DIAMOND FIRE
1542—GUILTY

HARLEQUIN ROMANCE
1631—MASQUERADE
1656—AUTUMN OF THE WITCH

ANNE MATHER

Dangerous Sanctuary

Harlequin Books

TORONTO • NEW YORK • LONDON
AMSTERDAM • PARIS • SYDNEY • HAMBURG
STOCKHOLM • ATHENS • TOKYO • MILAN
MADRID • WARSAW • BUDAPEST • AUCKLAND

Harlequin Presents first edition May 1993
ISBN 0-373-11553-9

Original hardcover edition published in 1992
by Mills & Boon Limited

DANGEROUS SANCTUARY

CHAPTER ONE

'I THINK that's all for today, Jaime.' Felix Haines got up from his desk to flex his aching shoulder muscles, grimacing when he saw his secretary's sympathetic smile. 'You can laugh,' he added, 'but playing squash twice a week is going to do me good. As soon as I master it, that is.'

'So long as it doesn't master you first,' responded Jaime drily, folding her shorthand notebook, and slipping her pencil into the metal spiral that secured the pages. 'Honestly, I can't see the sense of beating yourself to death just to prove you're still active! I'm sure you'd find it simpler to join a golf club.'

'Perhaps so.' Felix was a little irritable. 'But Lacey would think I was taking the easy way out—and I would be. As she says, forty-six isn't old. I've just let myself get lazy, that's all.'

Jaime reserved judgement on Lacey Haines's opinion. Since she'd broken up Felix's first marriage, and married him herself eighteen months ago, Lacey seemed bent on changing him from the easygoing middle-aged man she claimed she had fallen in love with to one of those ultra-fit sporting types you frequently saw on television. Men with trim figures, and sharp, hungry faces, men who Jaime privately thought were striving desperately to hang on to their youth. Talk about women being the vainer sex, she mused, watching Felix, as he endeavoured to throw off the stiffness of over-worked muscles. Still, Lacey was more than fifteen years his junior, so perhaps he felt compelled to make the effort.

'Haven't you ever thought of joining a keep-fit group?' Felix asked now, as Jaime rose from her seat and began walking towards the door that led into her office. 'Lacey goes to an aerobics class every Wednesday. You should join her.'

5

'Oh, I—don't think so,' said Jaime finally, softening her refusal with a rueful smile. She could almost hear Lacey's reaction to a suggestion like that. Lacey had never forgiven her for taking Margaret Haines's side during the divorce proceedings, and if there had been any way she could have persuaded Felix to find another secretary she would have done it. But happily for Jaime, Felix was fond of her, and their twelve-year partnership had stood the test. 'I—er—I don't really have that much time,' Jaime appended now, realising belatedly that Felix might misunderstand her motives. 'I mean—what with Tom, and everything. I—just never seem to have a moment to myself.'

Felix regarded her a little dourly now. 'You don't like Lacey, do you?' he exclaimed, out of the blue. 'Oh——' he lifted a hand to silence her, as she opened her mouth to protest '—you don't have to say anything. I know. I'm not entirely without perception, Jaime, whatever you think. I just wish it weren't so.'

Jaime's tongue circled her lips. 'Felix, I——'

'You still see Maggie, don't you?'

'Occasionally.' Jaime nodded.

'And she's poisoned your mind about Lacey, I suppose.'

'No!' Jaime was dismayed. 'We never discuss your marriage, Felix.'

He snorted then. 'Do you expect me to believe that?'

Jaime stiffened. 'I think you flatter yourself, *Mr* Haines,' she retorted, reaching for the handle of the door. 'If that's all——'

'Oh, Jaime!' Felix sighed and came towards her, shaking his head. 'Don't look at me like that. All right. Perhaps I was out of line in suggesting you and Maggie spend your time pulling me to pieces. But you have to admit, it's not unreasonable to assume my name is mentioned!'

Jaime hesitated. 'Felix, my associating with Lacey—or rather the lack of it—has nothing to do with your ex-wife. Lacey and I just don't—get on. It's as simple as that. I'm sure, if you asked her, she'd say the same.'

Felix frowned. 'I suppose you know she's jealous of you.'

'Jealous of me?' Jaime was staggered. 'You're not serious!'

'I am.' Felix pushed his hands into his jacket pockets and rocked back on his heels. 'You're a beautiful woman. I've always thought so. And—who knows?—if you'd ever given me the slightest encouragement——'

'Felix!' Jaime stopped him there. She couldn't believe this conversation was actually happening, and she had no wish to complicate an already difficult situation. 'I think I'd better go...'

'Oh, don't worry.' Felix was amazingly casual about it. 'It's a few years now since I got over my infatuation. You made it abundantly clear, consciously or otherwise, that you weren't interested. Not in so many words, perhaps. But subtly. When you told me about Tom's father, for instance.'

Jaime felt as if she was totally out of her depth here. 'Felix, I told you about Tom's father because——'

'I know. To explain that Tom wasn't your ex-husband's son,' Felix assured her tolerantly. 'And I sympathised, didn't I? I never liked Philip Russell myself. But I also realised you were unlikely to let another man into your life for quite some time. Maybe not ever. And I didn't want to lose the best secretary I'd ever had.'

Jaime tried to keep calm. 'I—don't know what to say,' she murmured, aware that the idea of Felix—shy, be-spectacled, *sober* Felix—nurturing some unrequited passion for her seemed totally unbelievable. He had always struck her as being such a moderate man. But, she acknowledged drily, he had left his wife of some twenty years for a much younger woman, so who could tell what went on behind that bland façade?

'There's no need to say anything,' Felix reassured her, turning away from the evident confusion in her face. 'I knew you were unaware that I existed—in a sexual way, that is. You were too wrapped up with your own affairs to notice anything—or anyone—else.'

Jaime felt the hot colour invading her cheeks. So far, she had succeeded in controlling her intense embarrassment, but now she could hide it no longer. 'I'm—sorry,' she mumbled, jerking open the door, wishing he had never brought the subject up. Goodness, it resurrected too many other memories she would rather not think about, and she was glad to escape to the comparative sanctuary of her own office.

However, Felix's voice followed her. 'Anyway,' he called, and somehow she sensed his casual tone concealed a covert curiosity, 'talking of the Russells, did you know the old Priory had been sold?'

Steeling her nerves, Jaime came back to the open doorway. 'The old Priory?' she said, with commendable composure. 'What does the old Priory have to do with the Russells? Except that Philip stayed there years ago.'

'Wasn't it where you met your ex-husband?' Felix probed innocently. 'I seem to remember——'

'I met Philip in the bar at the Raven,' retorted Jaime levelly, feeling a sense of disquiet she had not felt for years. What was Felix up to now? Surely Philip hadn't bought the Priory.

'So, it wouldn't bother you, meeting him again,' her employer suggested mildly, shuffling some papers on his desk, and Jaime sighed.

'I suppose not,' she responded tightly, even though the prospect filled her with alarm. 'What are you saying? That Philip is the new owner of the Priory?'

'No.' Felix lifted his head, and Jaime had the distinct suspicion that he was enjoying this. Maybe he still resented her attitude towards Lacey, whatever he said. 'No, Philip hasn't bought the Priory, Jaime. His brother has.'

How Jaime managed to remain standing, she never knew. Felix's words had struck her with all the force of a body blow, and the desire to double up under its onslaught was overwhelming.

'You did meet Ben Russell, didn't you?' Felix continued, his expression mirroring none of the horror Jaime was feeling. She must be more skilful at hiding her reactions than she had imagined, she thought faintly. But on no account must he guess how she was feeling at this moment.

With her mouth dry, and her heart beating heavily in her chest, even the word 'Yes' required an immense amount of effort, but Jaime managed it. She even added, 'How interesting,' just for good measure, before stepping weakly back to her desk.

Then, *Ben*! she mouthed disbelievingly, propping herself limply against the scarred wood. Ben was coming to live in Kingsmere! Oh, God, it couldn't be true, could it? Fate couldn't be so cruel!

And yet, remembering the way it had treated her in the past, Jaime knew it could. In life there were no guarantees, no limits to the pain and frustration any one person could suffer. Even after all these years, it still wasn't through with her. She pressed a trembling hand to her throat as a wave of dizziness swept over her.

Then, realising that Felix could appear at any moment and find her in this state, Jaime struggled to pull herself together. It was quite late—almost four o'clock already. If she could just manage to get through the next half-hour, she would have a whole weekend to recover from the shock. Besides, she told herself fiercely, it wasn't as if they were likely to run into one another. If it hadn't been for Philip, she would never have met the other members of the Russell family. No, she and Tom were safe. Ben was unlikely to seek her out after all this time.

Even so, it had been a blow, and, despite the way he had phrased it, Jaime was pretty sure Felix had intended to disconcert her. But even he could have no idea of the emotional turmoil into which his careless words had thrown her. She guessed his only intention had been to get his own back.

Taking a deep breath, she picked up the papers she had been about to file when Felix summoned her, and was apparently calmly slotting them into their individual compartments in the filing cabinet when Felix put his head round the door.

'I'm leaving now,' he said, coming more fully into the room. 'When you've finished what you're doing, you can go, too, if you like.' He hesitated. 'You're not mad at me, are you?'

'Mad at you?' Once again Jaime called on all her reserves of strength to face this new challenge. 'Why should I be mad at you?'

'Well...' Felix shrugged '...that business over the Priory. Teasing you about Philip, and so on. I haven't upset you, have I?'

Jaime forced a smile. 'Don't be silly, Felix,' she declaimed, closing the filing-cabinet drawer with careful precision. 'Where any member of that family chooses to live is no concern of mine.'

'No, but——'

'Honestly. It's OK.' Jaime made a play of examining the remaining documents in her hands. 'Have a good weekend, Felix. And don't overdo the exercise. Remember the old adage: moderation in all things.'

Jaime suspected she ought to take her own advice later that afternoon, as she drove home through the fading light of a chilly November day. A brief stop at the supermarket had done little to ease her tension, and after fighting her way through the maze of shopping trolleys she was in no mood to face the delays caused by the roadworks in Gloucester Road. Why did they always start digging up the road at weekends? she wondered uncharitably, ignoring the fact that a burst water-main earlier in the day had flooded the road during the morning rush-hour. All she could think was that Tom would be home and waiting for his evening meal, while she was stuck here wasting valuable time—and petrol.

It was half-past five when she reached Dorset Road, and the small terrace house she shared with her fourteen-year-old son. Parking the car in the road, she got out and locked the doors, then collected the bag of groceries from the boot before letting herself into the house.

'Tom!' she called, as she slammed the front door behind her. 'Tom? Where are you?'

'I'm up here, Mum.' Her son's voice came from the top of the stairs and, looking up, Jaime saw him silhouetted against the light streaming out of his bedroom behind him. 'Angie's helping me with my homework.' He paused, and then added innocently, 'Did you have a good day?'

Jaime beat back the retort that sprang to her lips, and grimaced. 'It was OK,' she acknowledged tautly, aware that Tom's question had more to do with her reaction to finding Angie Santini in the house than any real interest in her occupation. He knew her feelings about his friendship with the Italian girl, and he was effectively blocking any protest she might be about to make.

'Your meal will be on the table in fifteen minutes,' Jaime said now, continuing down the hall. It was a tacit request that Angie be out of the house in the same length of time, and Tom turned back into his room, evidently understanding her unvoiced command.

Unpacking the things she had bought on to the table in the kitchen, Jaime endeavoured not to allow her own feelings of anger and resentment to exaggerate the importance of finding Angie Santini in Tom's bedroom. It wasn't as if they were doing anything wrong, she argued to herself. She trusted Tom, and it was true he was having some trouble understanding the complicated problems the maths masters were presently giving them. It was also true that Angie, for all her promiscuity, was good at maths. And, if it had been anyone else, even another girl, she doubted she would have given it a second thought. But it wasn't. It was Angie Santini, and Jaime didn't like it.

She sighed. Angie—or Angela, to give her her proper name—always seemed so much older than Tom. Even though they were both in the same year at the local comprehensive, Angie never acted like Jaime's idea of a fourteen-year-old. Perhaps Italian girls matured that much sooner, Jaime reflected, turning on the grill, and spreading two thick slices of gammon on the tray. And Tom, who was so young and immature in some ways, was tall for his age. He was the natural choice for someone with Angie's undoubted sensuality: thin, and athletic, and physically attractive. He had always inspired interest, even when he was younger. Like his father, thought Jaime bitterly, viciously jabbing a fork into the skins of the potatoes she was putting into the microwave oven. He had his father's unique air of individuality, his lazy charm, and physical grace. But thankfully not his colouring, Jaime appended grimly. In fact, Tom didn't even look like his father. His silky blond hair and sensitive features were peculiarly Jaime's, a circumstance for which she never ceased to be grateful. Because of that, she had been able to return to Kingsmere secure in the knowledge that no one could point a finger at either of them.

'Angie's leaving now, Mum.'

Lost in thought, Jaime had been unaware of the two young people descending the stairs, but now Tom's voice alerted her to the fact. 'What—oh, yes. Goodbye, Angie,' she said, fighting her dislike. And added, for Tom's sake, 'Nice to see you again.'

'Nice to see you, too, Mrs Russell.' Angie's English was perfect, due to the fact that her parents had moved to England soon after she was born. 'You look tired. Did you have a hard day?'

Jaime's smile was thin, but determined. 'Something like that,' she murmured, immediately convinced she must look as harassed as she felt. Angie, on the other hand, looked as fresh and exotic as an orchid, the dark hair tumbling about her shoulders accentuating her alien beauty. The jeans and jacket she was wearing only added to her voluptuous appearance, and Jaime was reluctantly aware of how flattered Tom must feel to be the object of her attentions.

'I thought you said it was OK,' Tom put in now, and it took Jaime a minute to realise he was talking about her day.

'Oh—you know me,' she demurred, smelling the gammon and using it as an excuse to turn back to the grill. 'Hurry home, Angie.'

'I've said I'll walk her to the corner,' said Tom, lifting his parka from the row of hooks behind the front door, and sliding his arms into the sleeves.

Jaime bit her tongue on the protest she wanted to make, and merely nodded. You were young once, she reminded herself severely, taking a pack of frozen peas out of the freezer. You were only eighteen when you married Philip Russell, and no one could stop you. But all the same, fourteen still seemed awfully young, and she had hoped that Tom wouldn't make her mistakes.

By the time Tom got back Jaime had the meal on the table. They usually ate in the kitchen when they were alone, and in winter it was a definite advantage. The central heating boiler was in the kitchen, and although Jaime turned off the radiators while she and Tom were out of the house the kitchen always retained its heat. Tom was generally home first, and he turned the radiators on again when he came in. Consequently, by the time they had eaten, the rest of the house was comfortably warm.

'What did you mean when you said you'd had a hard day?' Tom asked, smothering his baked potato with melted butter, and Jaime, who had hoped to avoid this particular discussion, considered a moment before answering him.

'Oh—my day was all right,' she declared at last. 'It—it was just something Felix said that—well, annoyed me, that's all.'

'What?'

'Don't speak with your mouth full!' Jaime used the reproof to reconsider her options. 'It wasn't important. Get on with your meal.'

'Well, if it wasn't important, why did you get angry?' asked Tom reasonably, wiping a smear of butter from his chin, and Jaime decided there was no point in prevaricating. Tom would find out soon enough. Someone was bound to tell him that his uncle was moving to Kingsmere.

'Apparently Ben Russell is negotiating to buy the old Priory,' she said, her offhand tone a warning not to pursue the subject, but Tom was too surprised to be perceptive.

'*Uncle* Ben?' he exclaimed, his jaw dropping, and Jaime wished she had just let him find out after all.

Now, she adopted an indifferent air. 'How many Ben Russells do you know?' she asked, avoiding a direct answer. 'Tom—eat your meal. It's getting cold.'

Tom frowned, but he wasn't diverted. 'Why is Uncle Ben coming to live in Kingsmere?' he demanded. 'I thought you said he lived in Africa, or somewhere like that.'

'Yes—well, he did.' Jaime endeavoured to speak casually. 'I don't know why he's coming to live at the Priory. Perhaps he's not. Perhaps he's just buying it as an investment.'

'The old Priory?' Tom looked sceptical. 'Mum, it's falling to bits. No one would buy that as an investment. It's been on the market for over two years!'

'Well, that's not our concern, is it?' said Jaime evenly, making a valiant effort to look as if she was eating her

own meal. 'So did you get your homework done? I hope
Angie's parents weren't worried about where she was.'

'Oh, they don't worry about her,' declared Tom airily.
'They know she's all right if she's with me. Besides,
they're too busy.'

'Hmm.'

Jaime thought he was probably right, though she re-
frained from saying so. The Santinis were unlikely to
worry about Angie in the same way she worried about
Tom. Angie had half a dozen brothers and sisters, and
besides, they had a thriving business to keep their
interest. Jaime had been into the shop the Santinis owned
on the precinct only once, but she had been left with an
impression of orderly chaos. The place had been filled
with customers, all wanting to buy the rich hams and
aromatic cheeses that the Santinis imported from their
home country, and the idea of Caterina Santini fretting
because her eldest daughter was late home from school
didn't seem likely.

'Anyway, do you think he'll come and see us?' Tom
asked now, and Jaime realised her attempt to distract
him hadn't worked.

'I hope not,' she replied, attacking her steak with renewed vigour. 'Is your gammon all right? Mine seems
a little tough.'

'Oh—yes.' Tom dismissed that diversion without
effort. 'I suppose it's not very likely, is it? Not after the
way Dad's treated us all these years.'

Jaime stifled a groan, and got up from the table to
dump most of her meal into the waste-bin. 'Do you want
any dessert?' she asked, without answering him. 'There's
apple pie. Or cheese.'

'Can I have both?' Tom scraped his plate clean, and
handed it to her with an angelic smile. Then, just when
she thought it was over, he added, 'Did you know him
well?'

Jaime's breath escaped with a gulp. 'I—met him,' she
temporised, taking refuge in removing the apple pie from
the fridge. 'Do you want cream?'

'Just cheese, please,' he responded irrepressibly. Then,
'Go on about Uncle Ben. Did he come to the wedding?'

Jaime made a helpless gesture. 'What does it matter?'

'Well, you told me my grandparents didn't come,' pointed out Tom, picking up his spoon. 'Dad's parents, that is. Why didn't they approve of you?'

'Because they had someone else in mind,' retorted Jaime tightly, unwilling to allow any thoughts of that kind to add to her frustration. 'We've talked about this before, Tom. You know the story. Now, can we change the subject?'

But he didn't know the story, Jaime chided herself, as she filled the washing-up bowl with water, and added a soapy detergent. And for some time she had been pondering the wisdom of letting Tom go on thinking that Philip Russell had been his father. But the alternative had always seemed so untenable, and, because he had been denied so much, did she have the right to deny him his legitimacy as well?

Now, however, the choice had been made for her. There was no way she was going to unsettle her son now that Ben Russell was moving back to Kingsmere. She wondered if his wife was moving back with him. Thank God there was no reason for them to see one another.

Tom finished his pie and brought the empty dish to the sink, watching as his mother submerged it in the water. 'I know you don't like talking about it, Mum,' he ventured, dipping his finger into the suds, and drawing an elongated circle. 'But it was a long time ago, wasn't it? Don't you think it's time you could talk about it without getting upset?'

'I'm not upset.' Jaime stiffened defensively. 'I just don't see why you want to labour the point. I was just the publican's daughter, and your—your—the *Russells*— wanted their son to marry someone from their own level of society. Someone with money, and position. It's a common enough story, goodness knows. Philip soon realised his mistake, and—and so did I.'

Tom grimaced. 'Leaving you holding the baby!'

'In a manner of speaking.' Jaime thrust a tea-cloth into his hands, and indicated the draining dishes. 'Come on. Make yourself useful.'

'I still don't understand,' muttered Tom, taking the tea-cloth and starting to dry the plates. 'If he was planning on leaving us, why did he wait until you were expecting a baby?'

'Oh, Tom, things happen that way sometimes.' Jaime's nerves were beginning to stretch. 'If I'd known telling you about the Priory was going to provoke this kind of discussion, I wouldn't have said anything.'

'I bet Grandpa knows,' said Tom shrewdly, and Jaime caught her breath.

'Yes,' she said, suddenly understanding all the little worried glances her parents had exchanged the previous weekend. 'Yes, I imagine he does,' she added, realising that as landlord of the Raven and Glass, which wasn't far from the Priory, it was virtually impossible for him not to have done so.

'I wonder if he'll come into the pub,' persisted Tom, thoughtfully. 'The way my father used to.'

'I shouldn't think so.' Jaime was short. 'Public bars are not Ben Russell's sort of place.' Or they weren't, she amended silently. She walked briskly across the room, and opened the door. 'I'll be in the living-room, if you want me. By the way, you didn't say—did you finish your homework?'

'Oh, yes.' Tom's grin was infectious. '*We* finished it. Angie's a real brain when it comes to figures.'

'Hmm.' Jaime was unimpressed. 'Well, just remember, Angie won't be around when you have to sit your examinations.'

'I know.' Tom's tone was faintly resentful now. 'I'm not a complete idiot!'

Jaime shrugged. 'Oh, well, I suppose it will give you more time for other subjects.'

'Not tonight.' Tom was indignant.

'Why not tonight?'

Tom finished drying the dishes, and hung the tea-cloth over the rim of the sink. 'Well,' he said, and Jaime could tell he was searching for the right words, 'I thought I might go to the disco at the youth club. It's only fifty pence, and all the gang will be there.'

'All the gang?' echoed Jaime drily, silently amending the word 'gang' to Angie Santini. 'Oh——' she gave a dismissive gesture '—if you feel you can afford the time, go ahead. But don't be late back. I want an early night.'

'Oh, Mum!' Tom's young face mirrored his disappointment. 'It is Friday night. How early?'

Jaime considered. 'Ten-ish.'

'Ten-ish!' Tom groaned. 'It doesn't get warmed up until half-past nine!'

Jaime wanted to be strict, but she knew half her impatience stemmed from her reaction to the news of Ben Russell's imminent arrival in Kingsmere. 'All right,' she relented, realising it wasn't fair to make Tom the brunt of her frustration. 'Half-past ten, then. But no later. And I shall expect you to do some work tomorrow.'

'Thanks, Mum.' Tom's relief was fervent, and he came to kiss her cheek with unexpected affection. 'You put your feet up, and take it easy,' he added, causing Jaime to pull a wry face. 'I'll help you with the housework in the morning.'

It wasn't quite the work Jaime had in mind, but she didn't argue with him. Nevertheless, it was only eighteen months until his important examinations, and she hoped this infatuation with Angie Santini was not going to jeopardise his chances of success. It was important that he do well. Important that he go into the sixth form, and eventually gain a place at university. It was what she wanted for him. What she needed to rectify the mistakes she had made.

But after he had left the house Jaime found she couldn't relax. Even the gloomy economic forecasts on the evening news could not dislodge the feelings of apprehension that gripped her, and the televised comedy shows that followed had little appeal. Was it just a coincidence? she wondered. Was Ben's intention to buy the old Priory just an innocent development, or did it have a deeper significance?

But what? What deeper significance could it have? It was fifteen years since she had last seen her ex-husband's brother, and she had no reason to believe he ever wanted to see her again. Indeed, he had probably forgotten she still lived in Kingsmere. And if he hadn't, it was obviously of little importance to him. After all, he had lived in Africa for the last twelve years anyway, initially working for the news agency's overseas service, and then writing—both factual articles and novels—equally successfully. She was deluding herself if she thought this move to the basically rural surrounds of Kingsmere had anything to do with her—or Tom. Wiltshire was a big county. It was just pure bad luck that Ben had chosen to buy the old Priory.

CHAPTER TWO

JAIME was vacuuming in the living-room when the telephone rang. Half expecting Tom to come charging down the stairs to take it, she did not immediately respond. Then, remembering her son had gone to take a shower, she switched off the machine, and went to answer it herself.

'Kingsmere, 2794,' she said, wiping a smudge of dust from her nose.

She fully expected to hear Angie's husky tones in response. During the past six months, her son's association with the Italian girl hadn't faltered, and, although Jaime was still fairly ambivalent about the relationship, in many ways she had to admit that Tom had benefited from the liaison. For one thing, he was keener now to do well in his exams. Angie had told Jaime—and, of course, Tom—that she intended to stay on in the sixth form. She wanted to go to university, and what had once been something only his mother cared about had become Tom's prime objective, too.

However, this time it wasn't Angie. Although the voice was feminine, the tones were much more mature, and Jaime had no difficulty in identifying their source.

'Jaime? Jaime, that is you, isn't it? It's Lacey here. Felix's wife. How are you?'

'Oh—hello, Lacey.' Jaime grimaced at her reflection in the hall mirror. 'What a surprise! I'm—fine. How are you?'

'I'm very well.' Lacey gave a little, girlish laugh. 'Or as well as anyone can be who's just discovered they're going to have their first baby!'

'Really?' Jaime was surprised. Felix hadn't said a word. 'When is it due?'

'Oh, not for months and months yet.' Lacey seemed relieved at the prospect. 'The doctor says it will probably be a Christmas baby. Isn't that exciting? But it's early days yet.'

'Of course.' Jaime moistened her lips, wondering why Lacey should have chosen to ring her with the news. They were hardly friends. 'Well, congratulations! I'm very happy for you—*both*.'

'I knew you would be.' Lacey sounded a little smug now, and Jaime wondered whether she was supposed to relay the news to Margaret Haines. She could think of no other reason why she should have been involved. 'Felix would have told you, but I insisted on telling you myself.'

'How—nice.' Jaime bit her lip. 'Well, as I say, it's very good news, Lacey.' She took a breath. 'Honestly.'

'Oh, good...' Lacey paused '...because we're having a party to celebrate, and you're invited. It's next Saturday. Can you come?'

Jaime almost gasped. Since Lacey's marriage to Felix, they had given a lot of parties, but this was the first time her name had been added to the invitation list.

'Well, I——' she began, trying frantically to think of an excuse why she couldn't go, but Lacey was not to be diverted.

'I'd really like you to be there, Jaime,' she said, and, unable to see her face, Jaime had no way of knowing if she was sincere or otherwise. 'I know we haven't seen a lot of one another in the past, but I'm hoping we can change all that. After all, we are going to have something in common now, aren't we?'

'Are we?' Jaime couldn't think of a single thing, but Lacey was quick to elucidate.

'Of course!' she exclaimed. 'We'll both be mothers. Oh, I know things must have changed a lot since you had Tom, but I'd appreciate your advice all the same.'

Jaime winced. That sounded more like the Lacey she remembered. The barbed comment wrapped in the apparently innocent remark. She hadn't changed that much, if at all. Even so...

'Perhaps I could call in for a couple of hours,' Jaime conceded, with some reluctance. Felix was her boss, when all was said and done, and she had no real objections to being civil. She doubted she and Lacey could ever be friends, but the other woman was not going to be given the chance to say her overture had been rejected.

'Oh, good.' To her credit, Lacey sounded as if she meant it. 'About eight-thirty, then. You know where we live.'

'All right. Thank you.'

Jaime grimaced, but the die was cast, and, replacing the receiver, she became aware of Tom's bathrobe-clad figure seated at the top of the stairs. He was obviously as curious about the call as she had been, but, refusing to give in to his overt speculation, she walked thoughtfully back into the living-room.

Nevertheless, she was not surprised to hear his hasty descent of the stairs, and by the time he appeared in the doorway she had schooled her features to a bland indifference.

'Who was that?'

Tom was nothing if not forthright, and Jaime had to smile. 'You should have answered it yourself, then you'd have known,' she replied vexingly. 'What do you want for lunch? Pizza, or salad?'

'Need you ask?' Tom pulled a face, and then returned to his earlier question. 'It was Mrs Haines, wasn't it?' he added, revealing he had listened to most of the conversation. 'What did she want?'

Jaime abandoned the idea of continuing with the vacuuming for the moment, and sank down on to the sofa. Crossing one jeans-clad leg over the other, she said, 'She wanted to tell me she's pregnant. She's going to have a baby at Christmas.'

'I do know what being pregnant means, Mum,' said Tom impatiently. 'So what? Why did she want to tell you and not Felix?'

'*Mr* Haines to you,' Jaime corrected automatically. And then she shrugged. 'They're giving a party. To celebrate. I'm invited.'

'Why?'

Jaime laughed. 'That's not very flattering.'

'Oh——' Tom grimaced '—you know what I mean.'

'I know.' Jaime relented. 'But I'm no wiser than you are. She says she wants us to get to know one another.'

'Do you believe her?'

'I don't have much choice, do I? Felix is my employer. I can hardly refuse to have anything to do with his wife.'

'But what about Mrs Haines? The first Mrs Haines, I mean. Won't she think you're abandoning her?'

Jaime sighed. 'You do have the knack of stating the obvious, don't you?' she muttered. But all the same, he had a point. Margaret was going to wonder where Jaime's loyalties lay.

'Anyway, I think you should go,' declared Tom staunchly, perching on the edge of a chair. 'It might be quite good fun. And you never go to parties.'

'Oh, thanks.' Jaime regarded him indignantly. 'Might I remind you that for the past almost fifteen years I've had you to look after?'

'Nana used to offer to sit with me—heaps of times,' protested Tom at once. 'And now I'm old enough to baby-sit myself. But you still never go anywhere.'

'Never?'

'Well—only occasionally. I'm sure you could have had a steady boyfriend, Mum, if you'd wanted one. You're still quite good-looking, and you're not that old!'

'Gee, you'll turn my head!'

Jaime was sardonic, but Tom was not deterred. 'I mean it. Angie says she'd love to be as tall as you. She thinks you're really elegant, you know.'

Jaime gave her son an old-fashioned look. 'Really!'

'Yes, really.' Tom was defensive now. 'What about Mr Price from school? He was really keen, but you just froze him off.'

'I didn't freeze him off——'

'Well, what would you call it? He asked you out *four* times, and you went once!'

'Mr Price isn't my type.'

'What is your type, then? Someone like Dad? Someone like Uncle Ben?'

'No!'

Jaime got up from the couch abruptly, and reached for the vacuum cleaner. She should have realised the way the discussion was heading. It might be almost six months since Felix had exploded his bombshell about Ben's buying the Priory, but she was aware that Tom hadn't forgotten, any more than she had.

Her father hadn't helped. Once he knew that she knew about Ben's plans, he had apparently assumed that there was no point in avoiding the subject. Even though Jaime's mother had evidently not agreed with him, Mr Fenner's attitude was one of dogged resolution.

'It's no use our Jaime thinking that, if she doesn't mention it, it'll go away,' he declared, when his wife first tackled him on the matter. 'In a small place like Kingsmere, it's news.'

'Well, it's not news I want to hear,' retorted Mrs Fenner shortly. 'And I'd have thought you'd have had more sense than to bring that man's name up when young Tom is around.'

'Why?' Jaime's father was belligerent. 'Do you want the lad to begin to think there's something funny going on? Because he will if our Jaime acts like Ben Russell doesn't exist.'

Of course, Jaime knew her father was right. A man with Ben's reputation—his fame—was bound to cause a stir in a place like Kingsmere. The fact that he hadn't actually come to live here yet was a small consolation. The renovations he was having done to the derelict Priory were what was causing the delay. But if what public opinion said was true, the old house was going to be quite a show-place, when the builders and interior decorators were finished with it.

The trouble was, Tom was intensely interested in the man he regarded as his uncle. Just last Sunday, when Jaime and her son had gone to her parents' home for lunch, he had been asking questions about the prospective tenant of the Priory, and Mr Fenner hadn't hesitated about elaborating on the extensive renovations that were going on.

'As I understand it, they're almost finished,' Jaime's father said, helping himself to more of the crispy roast potatoes that were his daughter's contribution to the meal. 'Bill—Bill Lewis, that is, who's been landscaping the garden—he says that a London firm of interior designers left several days ago, and as far as he knows the place is virtually ready for occupation. Of course, there's still some carpets to lay, that sort of thing. But my guess is that Russell will be moving in any day now.'

'I don't think we want to hear about that, Ray,' Jaime's mother exclaimed impatiently, but his grandfather's words had spiked Tom's interest.

'I do,' he declared staunchly, ignoring his mother's look of disapproval. 'I mean, we are related, aren't we?'

'We're not,' retorted his grandmother, giving her husband a quelling look. 'Now, have we all finished?'

Tom pursed his lips. 'But they are *my* relations,' he insisted. 'You never know, Uncle Ben might want to see me.'

'I don't think that's at all likely,' averred his mother, gathering the dirty dishes together. Then, aware of her son's resentment, she sighed. 'Tom, forget about Ben Russell. I wish to heaven he'd never decided to move to Kingsmere.'

'Well, he has,' said Tom sulkily, and even Mr Fenner looked a little discomfited now.

'I think you should do as your mother says,' he remarked, apparently losing his appetite for the extra roast potatoes. 'If the Russells had wanted to keep in touch, they wouldn't have left it fifteen years——'

'Ray!' His wife glared at him. 'Just leave it, will you? I think you've said enough.'

Of course, Tom had brought the subject up again on their way home. But Jaime had managed to evade his most personal questions. She tried to tell herself it was natural that he should be curious about his father's family, but, having lived for so many years believing herself free of the Russells' influence, it was unnerving to discover how mistaken she had been. As long as Tom believed that Philip Russell was his father, the connection—however tenuous—would continue to rankle.

Now, however, Tom evidently decided not to pursue his probing. His mother's withdrawn expression warned of an uncertain temper, and after scuffing his bare toes against the carpet he got up and left the room.

Meanwhile, Jaime restarted the vacuum cleaner with some frustration. How long was this going to go on? she wondered irritably. Was Ben's name to become an integral part of their conversation? It wasn't Tom's fault, of course. He was not to blame for what had happened.

But how was she going to cope with this nagging complication in their lives?

By the following Saturday evening, Jaime was wishing she had had the guts to refuse Lacey's invitation. She simply wasn't in the mood for a party. Although her relationship with Tom seemed as good as ever, she was unhappily aware that the problem with Ben was not going to go away, and it soured everything she did. On top of that, after spending the day catching up on her housework, she felt tired. Physically tired, she told herself, refusing to admit that it wasn't as simple as that.

Returning to her bedroom after taking a shower, Jaime viewed her pale face and wet hair without enthusiasm. She should have made an appointment at the hairdresser, she acknowledged, plugging in the hairdrier. But hairdressers were expensive, and she was used to doing her own hair. Fortunately, it was fairly easy to handle. Thick and wavy, and silvery blonde in colour, it used to be the envy of her friends. In her teens, its silky curtain had reached halfway down her back, but these days she kept it much shorter. A monthly trim caused it to curl quite satisfactorily into her nape, and she seldom noticed how attractive it looked.

With her hair dry, she considered her face with equal criticism. At thirty-three, she had grown accustomed to the singular composition of her features, and the high cheekbones, widely set eyes, and generously curved mouth aroused no sense of gratification. She looked what she was, she always thought: a working housewife, with little time to spend on either her clothes or her appearance.

Leaning forward, she smoothed a thoughtful hand over the skin below her eyes. She didn't have too many wrinkles, she reflected, but that was probably because the skin was stretched so tautly over her bones. She could do with losing some weight, but if she did she would probably look a hag. As it was, a hip measurement of thirty-eight inches would allow Lacey to chide that Jaime was letting herself go. Still...

Of the few items in her wardrobe suitable for such an occasion, a tan-coloured silk jersey seemed the most appropriate. With luck, it would not be a terribly formal affair, and the wrap-over neckline and button-through style gave it an indeterminate purpose. In addition to which the sleeves were long, which meant she didn't have to wear a coat. It was a warm evening, and with swinging gold earrings in her ears, and a handful of chunky bracelets on her wrist, she thought she looked ready for anything.

Tom whistled appreciatively when she came downstairs. 'You look great, Mum,' he said admiringly, and Jaime wished she didn't have the suspicion that his admiration was tempered by the fact that Angie's parents had invited him to their home for supper. 'You know, I bet if Dad could see you now he'd regret he ever walked out on you!'

Jaime let the comment go, acknowledging she would have to put up with her son's present preoccupation with his paternal forebears. It would pass, she told herself. It had to. Once the initial excitement of Ben's moving to Kingsmere died down, Tom would probably forget all about him. There was nothing like indifference to dull enthusiasm, and when it became apparent that Ben wasn't interested in them Tom's curiosity would wane. Perhaps her father was right. If she persistently questioned his attitude, Tom might begin to wonder. He was an intelligent boy. He must already have his own ideas about what had caused his parents to separate, and continually suppressing his enquiries could work against her. She would just have to go along with his comments, and hope that time would achieve what she couldn't.

Now, issuing Tom with final instructions about locking the door before he left, she bade him goodbye, and went out to her car. She was aware that several of her neighbours' curtains twitched as she crossed the pavement, and she guessed her unusually smart appearance was already attracting some comment. But still, she thought, tucking her long legs beneath the wheel, it was good to dress up now and then.

Lacey Haines met her at the door of the bungalow Felix had bought immediately after his second marriage. Large, and impressive, it stood in its own half-acre of garden at the head of a cul-de-sac. The cul-de-sac itself was part of the Lister Estate, a small community of luxury homes on the outskirts of the town. Jaime had never been there before, but there was no mistaking its identity. Apart from the many cars parked in the driveway and overflowing into the road, the sounds of music and conversation were distinctly audible.

'Oh—Jaime,' said Lacey, as she opened the door to her guest, and Jaime got the distinct impression that her presence was no longer so welcome. She didn't flatter herself that her appearance was responsible for the change in Lacey's attitude. Felix's second wife was everything Jaime was not. Small, and slim, and vivacious, Lacey could hold her own in any company, Jaime was sure. The sequinned jacket she was wearing alone would have kept Jaime and her son in groceries for some considerable time, and, despite the fact that Felix had told her that Lacey was suffering the early effects of her pregnancy, she looked every bit as self-assured as ever.

'I'm so glad you could come,' she added now, moving aside so that Jaime could enter. 'Come in. Felix is about somewhere. I'll get him to introduce you to everybody.'

So much for Lacey's wanting them to be friends, thought Jaime drily, stepping into the wide hallway that was being used as a reception area. 'Please, don't bother,' she murmured, observing Peter Manning and his wife not far away. Peter Manning was the manager of the accounts department, and a friend. Assuring Lacey she could cope, she headed in their direction.

'I didn't expect to see you here,' remarked Peter frankly, after they had exchanged greetings, and Jaime returned his rueful grin.

'Neither did I,' she confessed, smiling at his wife. 'But Lacey rang last weekend and invited me herself. And, in all honesty, I couldn't think of a convincing excuse.'

Marjorie Manning shook her head. 'Well, I wouldn't have thought you and Lacey had much in common.' She looked to her husband for confirmation. 'We only come to these gatherings because Peter's more or less obliged to do so. I feel awful about Maggie, but what can we do?'

'Nothing,' said Jaime firmly, accepting the glass of wine Peter had rescued for her from a passing tray. 'But who are all these people? Should I know them?' She indicated the crowded living-room beyond with the hand that held her glass. 'I didn't realise Felix had so many friends.'

'He doesn't,' declared Peter flatly. 'Most of these people are friends or associates of Lacey's. From the amateur dramatic society, most of them. Don't you recognise Gil Fleming, the male lead? And there's Stephanie Collins. She's usually his leading lady.'

'Hmm.' Jaime sipped her wine. 'Well, I'm afraid I don't go to the theatre very often.' She shrugged. 'But Lacey has certainly pushed the boat out. Do you think Maggie knows about the baby?'

'Knowing Lacey, I'd say it was a definite possibility,' answered Marjorie, with a grimace. 'Imagine Felix being a father again, after all these years!'

'Who's taking my name in vain?'

The subject of their discussion suddenly appeared behind Jaime, insinuating himself into their circle, and giving his secretary a challenging look. For some reason, his glance reminded Jaime of that scene at the office several months ago, and the embarrassment she had felt then stained her cheeks anew.

'We were just commenting on the fact that you're about to embark on fatherhood again,' said Peter quickly, leaping to what he thought was Jaime's defence. 'How long is it since your youngest was born? Twenty years?'

'Nineteen, actually,' admitted Felix, without rancour, and to Jaime's relief he switched his attention away from her. 'I know, I know. I'll be more like its grandfather than its father. But it's what Lacey wants, and that's what matters.'

'Of course.'

Marjorie's tone was dry, and Felix acknowledged it with a wry smile. But then, turning back to Jaime, he manoeuvred her into a position where only she could hear what he had to say. 'I suppose you disapprove, too,' he remarked softly, bending his head so that he could inhale the clean fragrance of her hair. 'What's the matter? Does it remind you of what you've missed?'

Jaime caught her breath. 'No.'

'Oh, well...' Felix shrugged '...I suppose you're feeling a bit miffed because he isn't here.'

'Who isn't here?'

'Although after the way you reacted that day when I told you he was coming back, I'd have thought you'd be relieved.'

Jaime blinked. 'I beg your pardon?'

'Don't pretend you don't know what I'm talking about.'

'I don't.' Jaime was confused. 'I thought we were talking about the baby.'

Felix gave her a doubting look. 'You mean Lacey didn't tell you?'

'Tell me? Tell me what?'

'That she invited Russell here this evening? He's in the neighbourhood, you know. I believe he's staying at the Crown while the final adjustments are made at the house.'

Jaime was glad of the press of people around her to support her suddenly unsteady legs. 'You mean—Ben?' she echoed faintly, realising something was expected of her, and Felix nodded.

'She didn't tell you?'

Jaime swallowed, managing to control her reaction. 'I—obviously not,' she articulated carefully. 'Did—er—did he say he would come?'

'He didn't respond at all.' To her relief, Felix didn't seem to notice how his words had affected her, and the noise and jostling of his other guests were a constant diversion. 'But, what the hell? There's enough people here as it is. Did you ever see such a scrum? Goodness knows what the neighbours must think, eh?'

Felix drifted away soon after that, and Jaime resumed her conversation with the Mannings. But his words had disturbed her, and every time there was a new arrival her eyes darted anxiously towards the door. But she needn't have worried. Although her nerves remained on edge, the man she had never expected to see again did not put in an appearance, and Lacey's hopes of achieving a social coup went unfulfilled.

Even so, it took some determination to swallow a couple of canapés, and exchange a few more words with her hostess. Lacey made no mention of her disappointment, and Jaime had to suppress a simmering sense of resentment. No necessity now to wonder why she had been invited, she thought bitterly. All that talk about motherhood, and being friends, had had an ulterior motive. She couldn't imagine why Lacey might think Ben would react positively to her presence, but she apparently had.

She managed to stick it out for another half-hour before making her departure. 'I don't like leaving Tom on his own for too long,' she excused herself, aware that no one here knew he wasn't waiting for her at home. In fact, she was glad he wasn't herself. She would welcome a few minutes to restore her defences.

It was only a quarter to ten when she turned into Dorset Road, and she guessed her son wouldn't be home much before half-past. Still, her appetite was returning now that she had left the source of her emotional upheaval, and she thought she might make herself an omelette for supper. In fact, Tom might like one too, when he got back. Although he enjoyed being invited to the Santinis', he wasn't too keen on Mrs Santini's cooking. Lots of pasta and spicy sauces did not appeal to her son's digestion, and he invariably made himself a sandwich after he got home.

To her surprise, however, the lights were on in her own living-room, and she knew a moment's anxiety as she pulled into the kerb. There was an enormous Mercedes parked directly across the road from her house, so at least the Morrisons were home, she thought gratefully. She might need their help if she had an intruder.

Of course, Tom could be home already, she reflected, as she got out of the car and secured the lock. Angie could be with him. But surely her parents wouldn't have allowed her to accompany Tom back to an empty house, she thought uneasily. Trust was one thing; putting temptation in their way was something else.

Her doubts were clarified, however, as she crossed the pavement. The front door opened, before she had a chance to use her key, and her son stood on the threshold. Tom's normally fair skin was flushed with colour, and Jaime's heart sank at the obvious connotation. They must have heard her coming, she thought, and decided to meet trouble head-on.

'You're early, Mum.' Tom's first words were not encouraging, and Jaime could tell by the nervous twitching of his lips that that was not what he really wanted to say. 'I thought you wouldn't be home for at least another hour.'

'No, well...' Jaime stepped past him into the hall, keeping her temper with difficulty '... it wasn't as exciting as you seem to think, and as you were on your own——'

'Oh—I'm not on my own, Mum——'

'No. I suspected that,' said Jaime tightly, watching him close the door with controlled irritation. 'How dare you, Tom? How dare you lie to me?'

'Lie to you?'

Tom looked blank, and before Jaime could sense the significance of his response another voice interrupted him. 'I'm afraid I'm to blame,' said the man, who had appeared in the living-room doorway. 'I suggested I might stay and wait for you.'

Jaime was glad she was standing by the banister. It gave her something to reach out and hold on to. Otherwise, she was quite convinced she would have keeled over, the shock of seeing Ben Russell was so great.

And it was Ben who had propped his shoulder against the frame of the living-room door. Of that, she had no doubt. But he looked very different from the way she remembered him, and she sensed that the years between had not been entirely kind.

Ben had been—*was*—the younger of the two Russell brothers, but right now he looked more Philip's age than his own. In height, there had never been much to choose between them, but Ben had always looked harder, more muscular, definitely the more *physical* one of the two, as a member of her father's bar staff had once rhapsodised. He certainly looked harder now—harsh, would have been Jaime's description. He was thinner, for one thing, and the thick swath of dark brown hair was lightly threaded with grey. His face, too, which bore the darkness of his years spent in a tropical climate, nevertheless showed a certain pallor—a sallow cast underlying his skin which pouched around his eyes. But his eyes were still as green as ever, a curious jade-green, that with their distinctive fringe of lashes had caused many hearts to flutter in the days when he had appeared on television. But, although she knew he must be thirty-eight now, he looked ten years older, and despite the chill of apprehension that had gripped her at the sight of him a reluctant stirring of compassion momentarily kept her dumb.

'Uncle—Uncle Ben came just after you left,' put in Tom stiffly, still smarting over his mother's accusation. 'I said you wouldn't be back until later, but—well, we got talking, and the time just seemed to fly.'

Jaime collected herself with a supreme effort. 'You mean, you've been here for the past *two hours*?' she exclaimed, trying to keep the panic out of her voice, and Ben flipped back the cuff of his leather jacket. In jeans and scuffed boots, he would have made quite an impression at Lacey's party, thought Jaime in passing. How ironic that he should be here, when she had been alarmed that he might turn up at the Haines's.

'To be precise, I'd say an hour and a half at most,' he replied tersely, after consulting the plain gold watch circling his wrist. There were hairs on his wrist, dark hairs sprouting up between his cuff and the strap of his watch, and Jaime's eyes were glued to them, as she tried to calm her nerves. 'I didn't mind. I had nothing better to do.'

Except attend a party that was supposed to be celebrating a baby's conception but was really in your honour, thought Jaime silently, resenting his assumption of control. 'I mind,' she stated, aware that her appraisal of him had by no means been a one-sided affair. She turned to Tom. 'Leave us, will you, sweetheart? I'd like to speak to—to—our guest privately for a moment.'

Tom looked troubled now, his earlier indignation giving way to a belated sense of responsibility. 'Don't be mad, Mum,' he said, giving Ben an appealing look. 'Why don't we all go into the living-room and talk? It—

well, it's not very nice out here, and Uncle Ben's been ill——'

'Do as your mother says, Tom.' Ben's quiet command silenced the boy, and Jaime knew a renewed sense of resentment at the ease with which he achieved his objectives. 'It's been a long time since we've seen one another, and I think it would be better if we had a few private words.'

Tom hesitated, but it was only a momentary resistance. 'You will say goodbye before you leave, won't you?' he requested anxiously, and then, conscious of his mother's disapproval, he dragged his feet along the hall to the kitchen.

Jaime waited until the kitchen door had closed behind her son before stepping back and opening the front door. 'I think you'd better go,' she said, hoping he was not aware that she was clinging to the handle as if it were a lifeline. 'I don't know why you came here, and I don't want to know. I just want you to get out of here!'

Ben's thin features tightened, but he made no move to obey her. 'Isn't this a little juvenile, Jaime?' he suggested, straightening his spine. 'We've known each other too long—and too well—to ignore the other's existence. All right. Maybe I shouldn't have come here tonight, but I was curious. And when Tom found out who I was——'

Jaime quivered. 'Are you going to leave, or must I call the police?'

Ben expelled his breath on a heavy sigh. 'You wouldn't do that,' he said flatly, his shoulders lifting in a dismissive gesture, and with an inward sense of desperation Jaime closed the door again.

'You have no right to come here,' she enunciated clearly. 'No right at all.' She took a steadying breath. 'Did you tell your *wife* where you were going?'

'Maura's dead,' he replied shortly, and now his face had taken on a distinctly grim expression. 'In any case, why should you think I don't have the right to see my own nephew?'

'He's not your nephew——' she began, but his savage words overrode her.

'Yes, I've heard that story before,' he bit out harshly. 'But if he isn't Philip's son, then who the hell is he? Because—my God!—the likeness is unmistakable! He's the image of my father as a young man!'

CHAPTER THREE

IT WAS strange, Jaime reflected, how the anticipation of disaster was sometimes worse than the actual event. In the early years, when Tom was just a toddler, she had lived in fear of Ben coming back and seeing the boy for himself. Even though Philip was no longer a threat, and the rest of his family had always lived in London, she had still looked over her shoulder every time she left the house, still felt the familiar tension every time the telephone rang.

But time had changed that. Time, and Tom's growing maturity, had convinced her that none of the Russells was ever likely to trouble her again. Why should they? She and Philip were divorced, and, because she had allowed him to divorce her, there had been no question of alimony, even had she wanted any—which she didn't. She wanted nothing from the Russells, not from any of them. And as the years had gone by she had begun to believe she was safe.

After all, Philip's parents had never liked her. She had known they had been relieved when her marriage to Philip broke up. That the reasons for that break-up might be different from what Philip claimed was not something they were likely to contemplate. But then, they didn't know Philip as she did, she reminded herself bitterly. As far as they were concerned he was still the shy, sensitive introvert, the image he presented to the world. The man Jaime had discovered him to be was someone they wouldn't recognise.

Nevertheless, when she had first discovered she was pregnant, she had been afraid that Philip might find out, and want her back again. The divorce had not been absolute, and she'd had no way of knowing how he might react. That was why she had left Kingsmere at that time, why she had gone to live with her father's sister in the north of England until Tom was born.

It had not been easy. Without funds, she had had to rely on her parents' support, but with their help she had managed. And, although those days had been anxious, they had been oddly satisfying, too. She had worked for a time, temping jobs, mostly, saving every penny she could for the baby. She had missed her parents, but she had asked them not to visit her until the divorce was final. She wanted no word of her whereabouts to get back to the Russells. Not until Tom was born did she begin to plan their future.

It was easier than she had thought. The fact that Philip already believed there was another man in her life made Tom's arrival quite unremarkable. Everyone—even her parents' neighbours—believed Jaime had left Kingsmere to be with her lover. That was why she had stayed away until Tom was almost a year old. Her return then had been greeted with the usual words of sympathy. People thought she had been let down, and she supposed she had, in a way, she thought dispassionately. Certainly, no one suspected her real reasons for leaving. Tom's presence answered a lot of questions, and if she did become the butt of some spiteful gossip for a while it was not something she cared too strongly about. She had Tom, and her parents, and that was enough.

Or so she convinced herself...

As the years went by, of course, her earlier impropriety was dismissed as a youthful indiscretion. By the time Tom was old enough to go to school, the question of who his father had been was no longer so important. She had retained her married name, and those people who didn't know her history naturally assumed that her ex-husband had been the child's father. Tom was no different from a dozen other children from one-parent families, and she had never corrected his assumption that Philip had deserted them.

Occasionally, she had worried that Philip might hear the fiction, and come back to see 'his' son, but it hadn't happened. Unlike the parents of Tom's schoolfriends, *he* knew that Tom wasn't his son—and besides, he had no interest in her now. The divorce had severed any remaining bonds between them, and he wasn't likely to resurrect the past.

Now, however, Jaime's carefully won anonymity was in danger of being overturned. As she had been afraid it might be, ever since she had heard that Ben Russell had bought the old Priory. But how could she have known he would come here? After fifteen years? It was obscene!

Even so, the bitterness of their last encounter could still bring a wave of goosebumps to feather her flesh. She despised herself for feeling this way, but it had been a traumatic evening, and she was vulnerable. God, was she never to be free from that one mistake?

'Shall we go into the living-room?' suggested Ben evenly, indicating the lamp-lit room behind him. 'At the risk of arousing your contempt, I am bloody cold!'

'Cold?' Jaime looked at him, becoming aware that in spite of the warm evening he was shivering. What was it Tom had said? That he was ill? 'I—all right,' she conceded tensely. And then, with a trace of malice, 'You usually get your own way, don't you?'

Ben looked as if he would have liked to argue with her, but self-preservation got the better of acrimony. Stepping aside, he indicated that she should precede him into the room. And Jaime did so, unwillingly, overwhelmingly aware of his lean body only inches from hers as she inched past.

Ben followed her into the room, and closed the door behind him. 'Shall we sit down?'

He gestured towards the sofa, but Jaime shook her head, choosing to stand by the empty fireplace instead. Her legs might be unreliable, but sitting down with this man would be an admission of defeat.

'Do you mind if I do, then?' he enquired, and at her curt shake of her head he subsided on to the cretonne-covered arm of the sofa. Remembering how many times she had chastened Tom for doing the exact same thing, Jaime was tempted to protest. But caution kept her silent. The fewer comparisons she made between her son and the Russell family the better.

Ben combed long fingers through his hair now, surreptitiously wiping his forehead as he did so. In spite of her desire to avoid any trace of intimacy, Jaime couldn't help noticing the hectic flags of colour high on his cheekbones. What was wrong with him? she wondered, angry at the surge of anxiety that swelled inside her. It crossed her mind that it could be something more serious than the simple cold she had suspected. But it was nothing to do with her, she told herself. Ben Russell's existence wasn't her concern.

'So?' He was regarding her with a steady, inimical stare. 'Tell me about it.'

'About what?'

Ben swore. 'Don't play games, Jaime. I'm not in the mood for it. You know damn well what I mean. Now—we can do this civilly, or not. It's up to you——'

He broke off at the end of this to give a racking cough. Shaking his head in a silent apology, he pulled a handkerchief out of his jacket pocket, and muffled the sound in its folds. For an awful moment, Jaime thought he was coughing up blood. But the linen remained reassuringly unstained, though her helpless swirl of agitation demanded some release.

'What's wrong with you?'

The words were wrung from her, and as soon as they were spoken she wished she could take them back. She wasn't interested, she informed her struggling ego. The last thing she wanted was for him to think she *cared*.

Ben shook his head, as if as reluctant to issue any information as she was to hear it. 'It's nothing,' he said, though that patently wasn't true. He shoved his handkerchief back into his pocket. 'I picked up a bug in Mogadishu.'

'Mogadishu?' Jaime blinked. 'But isn't that in—in——?'

'Somalia, yes.' Ben seemed reluctant to expound upon this statement, but Jaime's expression must have persuaded him that something more was required. 'I've been working with the relief agencies there for the past two years. I guess I must have picked it up in one of the camps. Now, can we——?'

'I thought you were living in South Africa!'

Jaime couldn't prevent the automatic rejoinder, and with a weary sigh Ben inclined his head.

'I was. But after Maura died...' he shrugged '...I needed something to do.'

'You had your writing.'

'Political thrillers?' Ben's expression was self-derisive. 'Hardly a reason for living, wouldn't you say?' His lips twisted. 'But we're digressing. And if you're hoping that by talking about my condition you're going to avoid talking about Tom, think again.'

'I wasn't. I——' Jaime felt a renewed sense of indignation '—I was curious, that's all.'

'Curious, hmm?' Ben's observation was dry. 'That figures.'

Jaime looked down at her hands. 'Why have you come here, Ben? My—my life is nothing to do with you.'

'Isn't it?' Ben regarded her through narrowed eyes. 'I might have believed that before tonight. But Tom shot that theory out of the window. God—and I was concerned about the raw deal you'd had at the hands of my family! No wonder you looked so sick to see me.'

Jaime tried to control her breathing. 'How—how did you know where to find me?'

'It wasn't difficult. Your number's in the phone book. You still call yourself *Mrs* Russell. I never realised how relevant that was.'

Jaime swallowed. 'It's not your concern.'

'Dammit, Jaime, don't say that! For God's sake, why didn't you tell anyone? It can't have been easy supporting yourself, and the boy! Why didn't you let us help you?'

'*Us?*' Jaime was sardonic now, but Ben didn't respond to her bitter exclamation.

'Philip should have been told,' he said, through clenched teeth. 'God knows, I had no idea he was still seeing you. The last I heard was that you had taken off with some guy you'd known before you and Phil got married. That was why he cut you off without a penny.'

'Oh, no!' Jaime couldn't let him get away with that. 'Philip didn't cut me off without a penny! I did that. I wanted nothing from him! From any of you! I still don't!'

Ben expelled a tired breath. 'All right. All right. Have it your way. You didn't want any help from Philip. But, for God's sake, the kid's his son!'

Jaime's shoulders sagged. What could she say? If she let Ben go on thinking that Philip was Tom's father, would he tell his brother? Would she be expected to allow Philip back into their lives, however casually? She groaned inwardly. How could she let her son associate with a man who...?

'And if I still deny that Tom has any connection with the Russells?' she asked.

'I wouldn't believe you.'

Ben's response was so vehement that she wanted to weep. 'You must know that Philip divorced me,' she began, but Ben wasn't having that.

'He hasn't seen him, has he?' he countered. 'I have. For God's sake, Jaime, why did you do it?'

Jaime turned her back on him. She had to think, she fretted. Never, at any time, had she expected to have to face a situation like this, and she simply wasn't prepared for it. Though she should have been, she argued. It was months since Felix had told her that Ben was coming to live in Kingsmere. But, even so...

'It wasn't because of us, was it?'

She hadn't been aware of him getting up from the sofa, but now the warm draught of his breath against the back of her neck warned her that he had come to stand behind her. Which was disturbing enough, without the shocking reality of what he was saying.

'I——' Her tongue felt riveted to the roof of her mouth, and blind panic flooded her being. Answer him, you fool! she told herself agitatedly, but it wasn't that easy. 'Us?' she got out at last, with just the right measure of scorn in her voice. Moving stiffly, she put some space between them before turning to confront him. 'I don't think even you can believe that!'

She had the satisfaction of seeing the faint contortion of his features at the contempt in her words, but if she thought she could dismiss his question without an answer she was mistaken.

'I think it's what *you* believe that matters,' Ben declared doggedly, pushing his hands into the pockets of his jeans. The action parted the sides of his jacket, exposing the open-necked shirt beneath, and the low belt riding on his hips.

And, although Jaime wanted to look anywhere but at him, she was forced to acknowledge his unconscious sexuality. He might be thinner than she remembered, and he might look haggard, but his physical appeal was unimpaired. 'Why don't you tell me the truth, for a change?' he persisted.

Jaime's breath caught in her throat. 'And you think— the truth, as you put it, involves you?'

'Oh, stop acting as if you didn't once care what I thought,' retorted Ben harshly. 'All right, it's been fifteen years. I don't need you to tell me that. I've lived every one of them too, you know, and, whatever you think, it hasn't been a picnic!'

'Oh—shame!' Jaime was openly sarcastic now, but Ben didn't even falter.

'You knew how it was,' he persisted grimly. 'You knew I'd never leave Maura. I told you. But that doesn't mean I didn't care about you, about what happened to you. God, you know I did!'

'Oh, stop it!' Jaime's hands clenched. She knew she was handling this badly, but she couldn't let him go on. 'I don't think there's any point in rehashing something that was—that was never anything more than a—a mild aberration, on both our parts,' she declared, hoping she sounded more convincing than she felt. 'I—was going through a bad time, and you were there. I was—grateful. But that's all there was to it.'

'Crap!' Ben's reaction was violent, and before she had a chance to take any evading action he had crossed the space between them, and clamped his hands to her shoulders. 'Don't bait me, Jaime,' he added, his hard fingers biting through the fine material of her dress. 'You might have been able to fool that crazy brother of mine, but I know you. Better than he ever did, I'd say.'

Jaime knew she must keep control here. Events were moving too fast, and the desire to escape those cruel, yet unbearably familiar hands was rampant. She knew she mustn't allow his anger to force her into any unguarded admission. It would be too easy to say something she would later regret. But with the heat of his body only inches from hers, and the raw male scent of his skin invading her nostrils, she was in danger of succumbing to any means to get away.

'Will you let go of me?' she demanded, resisting the almost overwhelming impulse to fight free of him. 'You can't browbeat me into agreeing with you. I'm not Maura!'

It was unforgivable, and she knew it. Throwing his dead wife's name at him like that was indefensible, and she was quite prepared for him to deliver an equally ugly response.

But, to her shame, Ben didn't say anything. He just looked at her, his green eyes searching her defensive features with stark deliberation. And, as he looked at her, his expression changed, the jade eyes narrowing and darkening in their intensity.

Jaime's resistance wavered. She told herself it was because she felt guilty about what she had said, but deep inside her she knew it was more than that. It might be more than fifteen years since Ben had held her and looked at her in quite this way, but in an instant her awareness of him was threatening to destroy all her hard-won independence.

And, as if sensing victory, Ben's eyes dropped to her mouth, to the vulnerable curve of her lower lip, and the pink tip of her tongue that appeared, and then darted nervously out of sight. His own mouth flattened, and the remembrance of how his lips had felt, moving possessively on hers, was suddenly an almost tangible memory. She remembered the first time he had kissed her as if it were yesterday. She remembered its urgency, and its sweetness, and the foolish belief she had had that he loved her. She had felt so protected in his arms—so *safe*. Had she ever been either?

But his reaction towards her was changing. She could see it. She could *feel* it. His hands were no longer bruising her shoulders. Their grip had become gentler, sinuously abrading the cloth, so that the silk jersey rubbed sensuously against her skin. It made her want to tear the garment from her flesh and let his seductive fingers do their worst, and when he looked down at the shadowy hollow, visible between the wrap-over folds of her dress, the blood started hammering in her ears. He was going to touch her; she knew it. Not as he was touching her now, but sexually, intimately, and there was not a thing she could do to stop him...

'He's mine, isn't he?'

The incredulous exclamation was like being doused in cold water. Jaime swayed, momentarily in fear of losing consciousness. Had he really said what she thought he had said, or was it simply a continuation of the crazy fantasy she had been indulging? She blinked, gazing at him through shocked eyes, and his hands, which only moments before had been caressing her shoulders, applied a bruising pressure.

'He is, isn't he?' Ben said again, harshly, accusingly. 'My God! Why didn't you tell me?'

It was difficult to think, let alone answer him. Jaime felt as if she had been standing on the edge of a cliff and someone had just pushed her over. She had the same feeling of precipitation, of being out of control, of having nothing to hold on to. Dear God, this couldn't be happening, she told herself. But it was.

'Mum? Mum? Are you all right?'

The tentative tapping at the door, and Tom's anxious enquiry brought her to her senses. Even if Ben's hands hadn't immediately dropped from her shoulders, Jaime knew she would have found the strength then to escape him somehow. Like a tigress protecting its young, she wrenched open the door, and much to Tom's surprise—and embarrassment—she pulled him into her arms.

'Of course I am, sweetheart!' she exclaimed, only allowing him to release himself with reluctance. But she kept a possessive arm about his shoulders, as she added with unnatural brightness, 'Your—your uncle was just leaving.'

Her eyes challenged Ben's to deny that, to repeat the accusation he had just made to her, and run the risk of alienating Tom's loyalties once and for all. But, of course, he didn't. As she had hoped—no, *known*—he wouldn't. Whatever he thought of her, Tom was the innocent party here, and Ben was far too shrewd to try to expose her to her son without proof.

'Oh, were you, Uncle Ben?' Tom asked now, shaking off his mother's arm, and giving the man a rueful look. 'Couldn't you stay and have some supper? I've made some sandwiches.'

There was a moment's silence, which for Jaime seemed to stretch into eternity, and then Ben made his excuses. 'I'm afraid not, Tom,' he declined, and although Jaime had been avoiding looking at him she couldn't prevent an automatic glance at his dark features.

But Ben's face was unreadable, the green eyes opaque between their thick veil of lashes. Perhaps he looked a little paler than he had done earlier, but she refused to believe that that was anything more than the vagaries of his fever. For he was running a temperature; she was unwillingly aware of that. Though her desire to ensure that he was looking after himself had suffered a distinct relapse in the circumstances.

'But we will be seeing you again, won't we?' Tom persisted, as his mother backed into the hall, and Ben came towards them. 'I mean, now that you live in Kingsmere——'

'Oh, yes.' Ben's confirmation was like the death-knell to all Jaime's hopes. 'You'll be seeing me again, Tom.' He smiled, but only Jaime noticed that it didn't reach his eyes. 'You can depend on it.' He paused, and then added, deliberately, 'After all, we are family.'

'Family!' Tom echoed the word with obvious satisfaction. He grinned. 'Yes, we are, aren't we? How about that, Mum? Even if Dad doesn't want to have anything to do with us, Uncle Ben does.'

Jaime felt physically sick, but she had to say something for her son's sake. 'I—I'm sure—Uncle Ben is just being polite, Tom,' she murmured, making a final bid to appeal to Ben's humanity. But it was wasted.

'On the contrary,' he said, 'I'm looking forward to showing Tom where I'm going to live. As you probably know, I've bought the old Priory, and I'm hoping to move in within the next few days. I've had quite a few alterations made, and I'm sure Tom would like to take a look at the gym and the pool-house.'

'An indoor pool!' echoed Tom disbelievingly. 'And a gym!' He gave his mother a bemused look. 'Holy shit!'

'*Tom!*'

Jaime was glad she could focus her anguish on something other than the man, who was so effortlessly baiting her, but her son was too excited to pay any attention to the reproof.

'I'll be in touch with you next week,' Ben promised, ignoring Jaime, as he passed her on his way to the front door. 'And apologise to your girlfriend for me, won't you? Tell her I'm sorry if I spoiled her plans for the evening.'

'Hey, no sweat,' declared Tom carelessly, as Jaime exclaimed,

'He doesn't have a girlfriend!' But no one was listening to her.

'It's been good to meet you, Tom,' Ben said instead, pausing at the door. 'You remind me a lot of myself, when I was young.' He offered the boy a grin which only Jaime knew was malevolent. 'See you—*both*!'

Jaime slept badly, when she slept at all, and she was up at six, making herself a strong cup of tea. Thank heavens it's Sunday, she thought, as she seated herself at the kitchen table, and wrapped her hands around the cup. She would have hated to have to go into work this morning and face Felix's inquisitive gaze.

Not that he was likely to know anything about Ben's visit. Not yet, anyway. But he would want to hear her opinion of the party, and it was going to be incredibly difficult to disassociate one from the other. The whole evening had assumed the trappings of a nightmare, with her own repulsive reaction to Ben's touch as the final humiliation. She should never have gone to the Haines's. She should have suspected there was more to it than a simple desire on Lacey's part to exchange confidences. But was that why Ben had chosen that particular evening to investigate her circumstances? Because he had known she wouldn't be there to obstruct him?

She shivered in spite of herself. Surely it hadn't been a concerted effort on all their parts to enable him to talk to Tom alone? she thought wildly. But no. She shook her head. She was getting paranoid. Ben hadn't even known her son was a Russell until he saw him.

But he had seen him now, she reminded herself tensely. He now knew what she had spent the last fifteen years trying to forget. That Tom was his son, not Philip's. That, far from being the child of some mythical 'other' man, Tom was his own flesh and blood.

Her hands trembled, and she put the cup down with a clatter. He didn't actually *know* it, she told herself fiercely. He suspected it. And she hadn't denied it—yet. But he had no proof. Nor would he have, if she had anything to do with it. But what was the alternative? That he should tell Philip that *he* had a son? God, no! She couldn't let him do that. She wouldn't give Philip that kind of rod to beat her with.

Unable to sit still, when every nerve in her body was screaming for action, Jaime got up from the table and moved to the window. Beyond the narrow panes, the walled garden spilled its fecund beauty, and she tried to calm her clamouring senses in its familiar surroundings. The previous year she had saved enough money to have the central area dug out and block-tiled, and now an upper level of trees and flowering shrubs tumbled over the retaining wall. There was a stone bird-bath in the centre, and a wrought-iron table and chairs, where she and Tom sometimes ate their lunch on summer weekends. It was small, but attractive, and her father had said it was the nicest-looking garden he had ever seen. But then, he hadn't seen the gardens of the Priory, she reflected bitterly. He was used to beer gardens, and pub yards, and the idea of sowing seeds or cultivating plants came very low on his list of priorities.

Jaime pressed her lips together. It all came down to what you could afford, she thought savagely. Until now, she had thought she had done fairly well by her son. He had been adequately fed and clothed, and given a comfortable roof over his head. And there had never been any shortage of love in his life. On the contrary, she had lavished all the love she had once felt for Tom's father on his son, making him her reason for living. She hadn't considered she was depriving him of anything. She hadn't even thought of the kind of life he might have had as a member of his father's family. The reasons for doing what she had done had seemed totally justifiable to her. But would they seem so justifiable to her son?

The unexpected sound of Tom's footsteps on the stairs threw her into a momentary state of panic. She couldn't talk to him now, she thought, looking desperately around the kitchen—but there was nowhere to hide. In any case, she had to face him sooner or later, and this was no time to be having an attack of nerves.

All the same, she couldn't help remembering Tom's ambivalence of the night before. It had been obvious that he couldn't understand why she should have such a dramatic aversion to his uncle's visit, and his own excitement at the prospect of pursuing the connection had vied with his usual loyalty towards his mother. The fact that she had refused to indulge his curiosity after Ben had gone had probably only fuelled his interest. She couldn't remember him getting up this early on a Sunday morning before, and feeling resentful because Tom wanted to see his uncle again was only playing into Ben's hands.

By the time Tom appeared in the kitchen doorway, Jaime had resumed her seat at the table. It seemed a more natural position to be in, and she assumed what she hoped was a casual expression of surprise as he came into the room. In his striped towelling bathrobe, with his hair rumpled, and the faintest trace of a soft stubble darkening his jawline, he suddenly looked exactly like Ben, and she wondered how she could have fooled herself all these years. Colouring wasn't everything, she acknowledged ruefully. Tom's resemblance to his father was more than physical.

But now was not the time to be having thoughts like these, she reminded herself grimly. If she wanted to keep her son's affection, she had to stop acting as if she had something to hide. She had to learn to play the game Ben's way—and that did not mean allowing someone who was a virtual stranger to come between them.

'Couldn't you sleep?' she enquired now, but her friendly smile was not reciprocated. For once, Tom didn't respond to her teasing, and her heart hammered nervously as he flung himself into the chair opposite.

'Couldn't you?' he countered, his blue eyes dark and accusing. 'You're not usually up this early either.'

'Oh——' Jaime lifted her shoulders in a dismissive gesture '—I was thirsty, that's all.' She indicated the teapot. 'Do you want some tea?'

Tom looked as if he might refuse, but common sense won out. 'Why not?' he said, and for all her anxiety Jaime recognised he was not as confident as he appeared. She must stop investing Tom with adult sensibilities, she thought impatiently. He wasn't Ben. He didn't have Ben's access to history. He was just a troubled child who needed reassurance.

Getting up from her chair, she took another cup and saucer from the cupboard, and poured his tea. Then, pushing it across the table towards him, she asked, 'What's the matter? Did I do something wrong?'

It was a calculated risk, asking him outright, but she was glad she had taken it when he said, sulkily, 'I don't know, do I? I don't know anything.'

Jaime sighed, resuming her seat. 'I suppose this has to do with what happened last night, hmm? You want to know why I—why I don't like Ben Russell.'

Tom looked at her over the rim of his cup. 'Yes, but you don't want to talk about it, do you?'

'I didn't. Last night,' conceded Jaime carefully. 'But I suppose I do owe you some explanation.'

Tom slurped his tea. 'It's up to you,' he muttered, and Jaime pulled a wry face.

'Well, either you do want to know or you don't,' she declared, her own confidence returning. 'And please stop trying to annoy me. You're not too old to be grounded, you know.'

Tom grimaced. 'I am nearly fifteen, Mum!'

'So?'

'Oh——' it was obvious Tom was losing his enthusiasm for the fight '—all right. So you can make me stay in. But that won't change anything, will it? I'll still want to see Uncle Ben again.'

Jaime's lips tightened, but she pressed them together so that Tom wouldn't notice. 'Well,' she said slowly,

choosing her words with care, 'I won't stop you. But—
I think you should know that when—when I was married
to—to your father, Ben Russell—assaulted me.'

CHAPTER FOUR

JAIME regretted those words as soon as they left her lips. Looking at Tom's shocked face, she knew she should have used a less emotive term. But what? What else could she have said? That Ben had attacked her? Which would have been worse, and wouldn't have been true. That he had forced her to have sex with him? *No!* Infinitely worse, and definitely untrue. And she had wanted to say something that Ben couldn't, in all honesty, deny. The fact that what had happened had been as much her fault as his was not something she intended to tell her son. She just had to give him a valid reason for not wanting to see Ben again. Her lips twisted. So much for her brave assertion that she wanted to tell Tom that Philip wasn't his father, she thought disgustedly. Like any animal, when it was cornered, her only desire had been to protect herself.

'He *assaulted* you?' Tom echoed now, his young face stark with horror. 'You mean—he *punched* you?'

Oh, the innocence of the young! thought Jaime painfully. Even in this savage world of sex attacks and pornographic videos, Tom still equated 'assault' with physical violence. But perhaps she ought to be grateful, she pondered. It could work to her advantage, and it was one way of defusing a potentially dangerous situation.

'Does it matter?' she asked now, neither admitting nor denying the charge. 'Suffice it to say my relations with that family have never been—normal.'

Tom frowned. 'But he actually—hurt you?'

Jaime tensed. 'Yes.'

'Well, what did Dad do?'

'Dad?' For a moment, Jaime was confused. 'Oh— you mean Philip.' She looped a silky strand of pale hair behind her ear with a nervous finger. 'Well—he didn't know anything about it. We—we were already living apart, you see.'

'And Uncle Ben blamed you, I bet,' prompted Tom, leaning towards her. 'No wonder you resented him coming here last night.'

Jaime couldn't believe it was going to be that easy. 'You understand why I was so upset, then?'

Tom nodded. 'I guess so.'

'And you appreciate why I don't want you to see him again?'

'Oh——' Tom looked taken aback '—well, he is still my uncle, isn't he?'

Jaime's jaw dropped. 'What do you mean?'

Tom looked rueful. 'It was a long time ago, Mum,' he said at last. 'I'm not saying I'll forget it, or anything like that, but he did come to see us, didn't he? I mean, he didn't have to. He could have just ignored the fact that we lived in Kingsmere, too.'

I wish he had! thought Jaime fervently, but she was learning it was safer not to speak her thoughts aloud.

'So—what are you saying?' she enquired, aware that there was an edge to her voice now that she couldn't disguise. 'That I should ignore the fact that he has no respect for me—*for us*?'

Tom looked uncomfortable now. 'Don't exaggerate, Mum. As I said, he didn't have to come here——'

'No, he didn't,' agreed Jaime tersely. 'Particularly not when he knew I was going to be out!'

That thought had just occurred to her, but she was sorry it had when she saw Tom's expression.

'Did he know that?' he asked, his eyes wide with speculation. 'Hey, do you think he really came to see me?'

Jaime wasn't sure how to answer him. She wasn't sure what was true and what wasn't. 'Well, he certainly knew Felix was having a party last night,' she muttered, wondering if Ben knew she worked for Haines and Partners. 'He was invited.'

'He was?' Tom was more and more intrigued, and Jaime felt like slapping him. He had no conception of what was going on, she thought frustratedly, over-looking the fact that that was hardly his fault in the cir-

cumstances. Her explanation—such as it was—had
achieved next to nothing. It would take more than the
knowledge that Ben had purportedly hit her to convince
Tom that he shouldn't get involved with any of the
Russells. In spite of everything, they represented
glamour, and excitement; and Tom's life was too
mundane for him to withstand the temptation.

Picking up the teapot, Jaime moved to the sink, and
tipped the rest of its contents down the drain. Then, rescuing the two used tea-bags, she dropped them into the
pedal-bin. A pile of ironing was waiting in its basket,
and the rest of the morning would be taken up with de-
frosting the fridge, and preparing Sunday lunch. Not
until all the dishes had been washed and put away would
she find some time to put her feet up and read the Sunday
paper.

It was not an appealing prospect, but until she had
come home last night, and found Ben seducing her son
with stories of handsomely restored mansions, custom-
built gymnasiums and swimming-pools, she had been
quite content. And she had thought Tom was, too...

'Did Uncle Ben tell you why he's come back to live
in England?' her son asked now, and Jaime realised she
would have to get used to sentences prefixed with those
two words.

'No,' she said, collecting the cups from the table, and
depositing them in the sink. 'What do you want for
breakfast?'

'He's been ill,' went on Tom, and Jaime thought it
was a measure of his interest in his subject that he should
put Ben before food. 'He didn't say much about it, but
I think he was advised to come back. He's been living
in a war zone for the past two years.'

Jaime's nails curled into her palms. 'I'm really not
interested, Tom. As far as I'm concerned, it's a pity he
didn't stay out there. Now—do you want to tell me what
you want to eat? Or aren't you hungry?'

Tom's brows drew together. 'It's early yet,' he
grumbled. 'You're not even dressed!'

'Bacon, or toast? It's all the same to me,' declared
Jaime, refusing to give in to his injured look, and Tom
hunched his shoulders.

'Bacon,' he muttered, finishing his tea, and then pulling a face because it was cold. 'If you don't mind.'

'I don't mind.' But his mother's tone was cool, and he knew it.

'Oh, Mum!' he exclaimed unhappily. 'Don't be like this. If—if you really don't want me to see Uncle Ben again, then I won't.' He scraped his nail across the grain of the table. 'It's no big deal. He probably won't want to see me again, anyway.'

Jaime wished she could believe that, but at that moment it seemed less important than reassuring her son. Looking into his troubled face, she knew she didn't have the right to stop Tom from seeing Ben, no matter what she thought. Tom was not to blame for her mistakes, and it wasn't fair to make him an innocent scapegoat.

'I'm—I'm sure he will want to see you again,' she ventured now, pushing her hands into the wide sleeves of her dressing-gown, and suppressing the feeling of resentment she felt at the sudden light in Tom's eyes. 'And—we'll just wait and see what happens, hmm?'

Tom blinked. 'You mean, you'll let me see Uncle Ben again?'

'If you want to.'

It took a great deal to say that, but Tom's reaction was compensation enough. 'I might not want to,' he said abruptly, confounding all her fears. 'I've thought about it, and—well, we don't really need him, do we? We've got Nana, and Grandpa, and Uncle David. He hasn't bothered about us before, so why should we care about him now?'

Jaime caught her lower lip between her teeth, as she felt the hot prickling of tears behind her eyes. Tom was so convincing, so loyal. He really believed, at that moment, that if Ben did choose to try to see him again he would have a choice. And he might, she conceded tensely, but knowing Ben of old she couldn't help having doubts.

But, 'All right,' she said, forcing a light tone. 'If that's the way you feel.' She squeezed his shoulder in passing. 'Now, I'm going to get dressed. You can wash up the cups while I'm gone, and I'll be back to grill the bacon. OK?'

'OK, Mum.'

Tom tipped back his head to give her a whimsical smile, and Jaime wished she could look at her son without seeing Ben's lazy charm in every move he made. It was such an unconscious thing. An unknowing sensuality, which made her realise why Angie Santini found her son so attractive. Funny, she had never noticed it before. Or had she simply been blocking any resemblance Tom might have to his father?

Whatever, Tom was a Russell, and there was no way she could pretend otherwise. He was his father's son, and she knew better than to believe that Ben wouldn't take advantage of the fact.

On Monday morning, Felix was eager to hear what she had thought of the party. 'Quite a bash, wasn't it?' he exclaimed, when Jaime came into his office at his request to take dictation. 'Lacey was quite exhausted yesterday. Which isn't like her, but I expect it's her condition, hmm?'

'Probably,' agreed Jaime, nodding, her own relief that Ben hadn't chosen to interrupt her Sunday making her less edgy. 'What time did it break up?'

'Around midnight, I think,' replied Felix, leaning back in his chair. 'But Russell didn't show his face, even though I know Lacey thought he might.' He grimaced. 'I guess we're pretty small-town for him.'

Jaime pretended to be adjusting her notebook, but when it became apparent that something was expected of her she shrugged. 'I—wouldn't say that.'

'Wouldn't you?' Felix regarded her consideringly. 'Well, you'd know better than any of us, I should think.'

'Why?' Jaime's indignation was not affected. 'Why should you think that?'

'Oh—you know.' Felix shifted a little uneasily. 'I mean, you have met him. *I* haven't. *Lacey* hasn't. It stands to reason that you know more about that family than we do.'

'Oh.' Jaime knew she should be appeased, but she wasn't. 'Well, just because I was once related to the Russells doesn't mean I'm in their confidence. In any case, I—I imagine it's a little early to be inviting him anywhere. Didn't you say he hadn't moved in yet?'

'That's right.' Felix was thoughtful. 'Yes. I'll tell Lacey what you've said. I know she was disappointed he didn't even acknowledge our invitation. But, as I pointed out to her, Ben Russell probably considers himself too good for the likes of us.'

Jaime sighed. 'What do you want me to say, Felix?' she demanded. 'That he does? That he doesn't? I don't know, do I? Perhaps you'd better ask him.'

Felix lifted his hands in a gesture of defence. 'All right,' he said soothingly. 'There's no need to bite my head off.' He paused. 'You don't think he'll come to see you, do you?'

Jaime kept her face impassive with extreme difficulty. Felix was fishing, and she knew it. But she had no intention of discussing her private affairs with him.

'I shouldn't think that's at all likely,' she declared, not a little disturbed by her capacity for lying. Had she become so inured in deception that she automatically chose the line of least resistance? 'I—hardly know him.'

Felix shrugged. 'Pity,' he remarked, picking up the first of the files lying on his desk, and studying its contents. 'Oh, well—I suppose we'd better get on.' He frowned. 'Is this all the information the Drummonds have sent us? I don't know how we're expected to make an accurate assessment of their tax liability if they won't provide us with copies of all their receipts.'

Jaime was relieved that Felix appeared to have abandoned his inquisition, and, applying herself to the job in hand, she put all thoughts of Ben Russell out of her mind. She had no doubt she would have plenty of time to think about him, and what he intended, in her free time. But, for the moment, she had better things to do.

And, in spite of her misgivings, it was amazing how swiftly the morning passed, when she stopped anticipating the worst. She had always enjoyed her work as Felix's assistant, and the intricacies of tax consultancy were a never-ending source of interest. She was always amazed at the lengths to which people would go to avoid paying their taxes—and she used the term 'avoid' advisedly. Tax *evasion* was illegal. Nevertheless, some of

Felix's clients were prepared to spend a small fortune in consultancy fees just to save what Jaime considered a paltry sum. Still, it kept Haines and Partners solvent, and she wasn't grumbling.

She drank her morning coffee with the girls who worked in the main office. They were a friendly group, and Jaime knew them well. One or two of the older women had been there longer than she had, though most of them were married, with families of their own. Happily, Felix was engaged with a client, and wasn't around to ask any more awkward questions. Jaime was not naïve enough to think he had said all he intended to say about Ben but, for the present, he too had other things to do.

The offices of Haines and Partners were situated near the town centre. At lunchtime Jaime often walked along to the High Street and did some shopping. She seldom ate much in the middle of the day, usually making do with a sandwich to see her through. Her mother was always saying she ought to make herself a salad to take to work, but Jaime replied that she didn't have the time. Which probably accounted for the extra inches she had such difficulty in shedding, Jaime reflected drily. It was all right Tom saying that Angie thought she looked good—if it was true. Italians liked their women shapely. Unfortunately, the current trend was towards the emaciated look, something Jaime knew she would never achieve.

Felix generally went home for lunch, but today Jaime didn't wait to see what he was doing. At half-past twelve, she picked up her handbag and left her office, eager to escape another tête-à-tête. Besides, it was Monday, and she did have some shopping to do. If Felix needed her for anything, it would have to wait until she got back.

It was a beautiful day. The sun was shining, and for once Jaime was not wearing a coat. But she considered her oatmeal linen, with its button-through style and cream silk camisole, sufficiently businesslike, and at least her arms were covered. Felix was old-fashioned about some things, and he preferred his secretary to dress conservatively.

She came out of the building, blinking in the bright sunshine, and for a moment she didn't recognise the man propped against the wall across the street. He was concealed by the shadows, and it wasn't until he straightened up and came towards her that she realised who it was.

Her immediate instincts were to flee, but she knew that wouldn't be very sensible. Besides, hadn't she been expecting this ever since he'd left the house on Saturday evening? She ought to be grateful he had chosen to speak to her while she was on her own. He could just as easily have made his accusation in front of Tom. And then . . .

But she refused to contemplate the alternative. She was a long way from giving this man anything that he could hold over her. He knew nothing. He was only guessing. But she must convince him that Philip need not be involved.

Ben looked less pale today, though the ravages that the past fifteen years had wrought were still harshly evident. Nevertheless, in an open-necked denim shirt, faded jeans, and the same scuffed leather boots he had worn on Saturday night, he was still worth a second glance. His hair needed cutting, she thought peevishly, wanting to find something about him that she could disparage. But the fact remained that he had always had the ability to stir her senses, and in spite of everything that hadn't changed.

'Hi,' he said neutrally, and she wondered if he thought he had a God-given right to come here and disrupt her day. 'Where shall we go?'

Jaime stared at him indignantly, and then, realising that if Felix chose to look out of his window he would see them, she started off along the street. Hopefully, if her employer did notice that she had a companion, he would not immediately assume it was Ben.

'Hold it!' Ben's fingers looped about her upper arm, effectively preventing her from going any further. 'My car's over here.'

'And why would that interest me?' asked Jaime crisply. 'I don't use a car at lunchtime. I can walk to the shops.'

'Later.' Ben's eyes were dark and impassive. 'We have to talk.'

Jaime breathed quickly. It was on the tip of her tongue to ask what they had to talk about, but the fear that Felix might come upon them was greater than her desire to be needlessly obstructive.

'All right,' she said, with what she thought was admirable restraint. Jerking her arm out of Ben's grasp, she swung about. 'If you insist.'

Ben gave her a twisted sideways glance. 'Did you really think I wouldn't?' he enquired cynically. 'Believe me, if I hadn't thought it might hurt Tom, you wouldn't have had more than twenty-four hours to prepare your defence.'

'*My* defence?'

Jaime felt the injustice of that remark sear through every fibre of her being. She didn't have to defend herself. Particularly not to him. Not after what he had done...

'I suggest you save your arguments until we're some place less public,' he countered, taking her arm above the elbow and guiding her across the road.

Jaime could see the Mercedes now, the same huge Mercedes that had been parked across the road from her house on Saturday night, and which she had thought belonged to someone else. It was parked some distance further along—on double yellow lines, she noticed irritably. If she'd parked there, her car would have been sporting a parking ticket by now, but Ben's vehicle exhibited no such proof of violation.

Still holding her arm—as if there was still some doubt that she might try to make a dash for it—Ben took out his keys, and pressed some sort of remote-control device that automatically unlocked all the doors. Then, with controlled politeness, he opened the front passenger door, and compelled Jaime to get inside.

'Do you mind?' she protested, to hide the awareness she had felt of those strong fingers. Although his grasp had been impersonal, her response to it was not, and the knowledge of her vulnerability was frightening.

He slammed the door behind her, as she struggled to jerk her skirt down over her knees, and walked around the car. At least the car was pointing in the opposite direction to the offices, she thought tensely. In spite of anything else, a car like this was inclined to attract attention. Not that it was particularly clean, she added, seizing on any topic to divert her from why she was here. The paintwork needed washing, and the inside of the car was littered with empty cartons, and scraps of paper. What was the old joke? she pondered nervously. Something about buying a new car, when the ashtrays in the old one were full. Yes. That was it. Well, that was probably Ben's attitude, too. She couldn't imagine him...

The engine fired, and she realised that while she had been concentrating on distracting herself Ben had taken his place beside her. The big car accommodated his long legs comfortably, and her averted gaze skittered over taut thighs and bony knees. Was all his skin as brown as the muscled forearms that jutted from the turned-back sleeves of his shirt? she wondered idly, before common sense suppressed such recklessness. It could be of no interest to her how he might look beneath the civilising influence of his clothes, and, although she had once found an intense pleasure in helping him shed them, that was before she had discovered the kind of man he was.

Her hands linked together in her lap but, feeling the way her fingers were abusing one another, she made a determined effort to calm herself. This was foolish, she told herself fiercely. She'd achieve nothing if she couldn't approach this situation with a belief in her own actions. She had nothing to be ashamed of. Nothing at all. For the past fifteen years she had made a fairly good job of caring for herself and her son, and just because Ben Russell had chosen to come back into their lives was no reason to doubt the wisdom of her actions.

Steeling herself to lift her head, she saw that Ben had negotiated the narrow confines of Moon Street, and was turning into Cheviot Road. His lean fingers handled the steering-wheel of the Mercedes with total confidence, guiding the big car as easily as he had guided her towards it. Of course, it had automatic transmission as well, Jaime noted sourly. Anyone could drive a car with automatic transmission. Even she could have handled it.

But reflecting on Ben's driving capabilities, however disparagingly, was not getting her anywhere. Observing his rather complacent expression, as he concentrated on the traffic, Jaime decided he probably thought he had intimidated her into coming with him. Well, she could disabuse him of that belief, at least.

'Where are you taking me?' she enquired now, relieved that her voice sounded more confident than she felt. 'I have to be back at the office at half-past one.'

Ben allowed her a swift glance. 'And you're never late?'

'No.' Jaime kept her eyes fixed on the road ahead.

'OK.' Ben braked, and pulled the car into the kerb. 'I guess this is as good as anywhere.'

'Here?'

Jaime was horrified. They had turned in to Gloucester Road as she was speaking, and now they were parked only a few minutes' walk from the comprehensive school Tom attended. Not to mention the shopping precinct, where the Santinis' shop was situated.

'Something wrong?'

Ben was lying back in his seat, regarding her with mocking eyes. He looked lazily relaxed, his fingers drumming a careless tattoo on the steering-wheel, and Jaime's hands clenched. Did he know where Tom went to school? she wondered. But yes, he must. There were only two secondary schools in Kingsmere, and he must know she couldn't afford the fees at Lister Park.

'We can't stop here,' she declared at last. 'We—we'll have to go somewhere else.'

Ben flicked a look at his watch. 'No time,' he said annoyingly. 'It's a quarter-to one already, and, as you said, you've only got another three-quarters of an hour.'

Jaime pressed her lips together. 'All right,' she said, through clenched teeth. 'I've got an extra half-hour. I'm due back at two o'clock, not half-past one.'

'Really?' Ben made no move.

'Yes, really.' Jaime gazed at him frustratedly. 'Look, can we move on? I—I don't want anyone to see us.'

'Like Tom?' suggested Ben drily, but to her relief he reached for the ignition. 'All right. We'll go to a hotel I know near the river. I don't know about you, but I could do with a drink.'

Jaime said nothing in reply. She was too tense, her eyes peeled for any sign of Tom, or any of his friends.

She guessed he might have bragged about his relationship to Ben Russell to his schoolfriends, and if he recognised the car...

But her fears proved groundless. The school lunch-break began at twelve-thirty, and by this time most of the pupils had dispersed. A lot of them went down to the precinct, she knew, but happily there was no sign of her son. He was probably already at the Santinis', she thought, finding that prospect less contentious than she might once have done. Compared to Ben Russell, her anxieties about Angie Santini seemed very insignificant.

The hotel Ben had chosen was not one Jaime was familiar with. Outside the town environs, it catered mainly to a business clientele, who used its gourmet dining-room to entertain their customers. It was nothing like the Raven and Glass, where Jaime had lived until her marriage, but it was exactly the kind of place she would have expected Ben Russell to patronise.

However, after parking the Mercedes on its spacious car park, Ben didn't go into the hotel. Instead, he directed her to follow him around the back of the building, where spacious gardens overlooked the shallow waters of the River Mere. Tables had been set out on a paved patio area, with pretty striped umbrellas, to protect those enjoying a lunchtime snack from the dazzling rays of the sun. It was all very smart and civilised, and, judging by its popularity, the beer was good, too.

Two men were just leaving a table, set at the far end of the terrace and, ignoring other, less private locations, Ben led the way towards it. Jaime, intent on assuring herself that she recognised no one among the diners, followed him less enthusiastically. Was this really where she wanted to engage in a personal discussion about her son? she wondered unhappily. Yet what alternative was there, short of inviting Ben back to the house?

A waiter appeared to clear the table of its residue of empty glasses and used ashtrays, and after he had gone, and Jaime was seated, Ben took the wrought-iron chair beside her. 'So,' he prompted, 'what do you want? They serve a reasonably good burger here, or you can have meat pie, or salad, or sandwiches.'

'I don't want anything to eat,' replied Jaime at once, adding a belated, 'Thank you' when Ben arched a quizzical eyebrow. 'I—er—I'll have a glass of lime and lemon. That's all.'

Ben, who had picked up the fast-food menu from the table, now gave her a resigned look. 'You must need something!' he exclaimed, dropping his eyes to scan the list. 'How about an omelette? They do have quite a variety.'

'I don't want anything to eat,' repeated Jaime, determinedly concentrating on the view. 'You—you have whatever you like. I'm really not hungry.'

'You're not dieting, are you?'

Ben's enquiry was accompanied by a studied look, and Jaime felt her colour rise. 'Why? Do you think I should?' she retorted, without thinking, and Ben's eyes met hers over the top of the menu.

'I wouldn't presume to answer that,' he told her smoothly, bringing a deeper blush of embarrassment to her cheeks, and Jaime fumed. Not for him the polite denial, she thought resentfully. Oh, why had she made such an asinine remark? He would think she was desperate for compliments!

The waiter returned at that moment to take their order, and Ben asked for a beer for himself, and a glass of lime and lemon for Jaime. He didn't order any food, however, and Jaime felt a twinge of remorse. She guessed he wasn't eating because of her, and guilt pricked her conscience. If he was just recovering from some illness, he probably ought to have regular nourishment, she reflected ruefully, before impatience stiffened her resolve. In heaven's name, she reminded herself, she hadn't invited him to come and spoil her lunchtime, had she? It wasn't her fault that he had chosen this time to interfere in her life once again. He could have waited until some more appropriate moment presented itself. He could have kept away altogether.

But the knowledge that he also could have come to the house again when Tom was there deserved some appreciation, and, much against her better judgement, Jaime pulled the menu towards her. 'Perhaps—perhaps I will have a sandwich after all,' she mumbled, following the list of fillings with her finger. 'Um—I think I'd like egg mayonnaise, if that's all right with you.'

Ben frowned. 'Why not?' he agreed indifferently, checking what she wanted, and putting the menu aside. 'One egg mayonnaise sandwich,' he ordered, when the waiter brought their drinks. Then, 'Cheers,' he added, raising his glass to his lips.

Frustration almost choked Jaime. 'Are—aren't you having anything?' she exclaimed, totally ignoring her glass.

'Not hungry,' responded Ben calmly. 'Now, if you've finished wasting time, perhaps we can get to the point of this meeting.'

'If I've finished——'

Jaime was on the verge of another defensive outburst, when a premonition gripped her. Of course, that was what he wanted. This whole exercise was designed to upset her, to put her at an emotional disadvantage. And Ben, who had once used his controversial debating skills to disconcert Members of Parliament and foreign diplomats, knew that better than anyone.

So, instead of indulging his ego, she broke off and picked up her glass. 'Cheers,' she murmured, raising it towards him, and had the satisfaction of witnessing his frustration instead.

But it was a fleeting glimpse at best. Ben was too experienced a tactitian to allow his feelings to dictate his mood, and, returning his glass to the table, he said quietly, 'Why didn't you tell me?'

There were any number of answers Jaime could have given, and she had spent long enough, goodness knew, considering all of them. Her first instinct was to pretend ignorance, to pretend it wasn't true—to offer him the story she had given Tom not so long ago. But Philip was Ben's brother, and that complicated matters. She didn't want Philip involved in this. She had no intention of allowing her ex-husband to muddy the situation.

'Jaime!'

Ben was waiting for an answer, and not even the return of the waiter with her sandwiches could delay it any longer. But she smiled at the man, and picked up one of the neatly cut triangles and examined its contents, before saying carefully, 'It was nothing to do with you.'

'Nothing to do with me?' Briefly, Ben lost his cool, and his eyes blazed angrily. 'I have a son, and you say it's nothing to do with me!'

Jaime took a determined bite of the sandwich. 'As—as you pointed out, you were married,' she declared doggedly. 'You ought to be grateful. I could have told Maura.'

Ben's lips twisted. 'That bugged you, did it? That I refused to leave my wife?'

'Bugged me?' Jaime could stand his baiting tongue no longer. 'Well, yes,' she said angrily. 'Yes, I think you could say that. It's not very flattering to hear that, although you're good enough to go to bed with, you're not worth sacrificing a perfectly good marriage for. Of course, I can appreciate that. I mean, I wouldn't have been as understanding if I'd found out my husband had been sleeping with someone else. But, hey! What do I know? I was just a diversion. A little bit on the side. And the fact that I was your brother's wife just added to the novelty!'

'That's not true.'

'It is true.' Jaime was into her stride now and, oblivious of where they were, or whether anyone else might be able to hear what she was saying, she went on, 'I believed you, Ben. When you said you cared about me, I really believed you. What a fool I was! Totally naïve! Well, we were both suckered, weren't we?'

Ben's face was grim. 'You don't understand.'

'Don't I? I think I do.' Jaime put the remains of the sandwich down, unable to even pretend she was enjoying it. 'Can you wonder I've tried to keep Tom away from the Russells? One brother a sadist, and the other a bastard!'

'You don't understand,' intoned Ben again. 'I couldn't leave Maura. She—needed me.'

'Needed you?' Jaime was scathing. 'How convenient! Is that how you usually absolved your conscience?'

'Usually, the situation didn't arise,' declared Ben harshly. 'What happened between you and me——'

'*Nothing* happened between you and me,' Jaime retorted grimly. 'Tom—Tom's conception was just a—a biological accident. I don't regard you as his father. I never did.'

'Well, damn you, I do,' grated Ben savagely, and then glanced over his shoulder, as if afraid his angry words had been overheard. 'Whatever kind of fiction you've managed to convince yourself of, Tom is my son! You can't duck out of that as easily as you ducked out of our relationship.'

'I've told you, we didn't have a relationship,' hissed Jaime angrily, leaning towards him, and then reared back in alarm when his hand moved to grasp the slim column of her wrist.

'I hear what you say,' he told her, in a low, dispassionate voice. 'But the fact remains, we did have sex together—more than once—and I got you pregnant, just as surely as we're sitting here exchanging insults!'

Jaime's breasts rose and fell with the tumult of her breathing. She was intensely conscious of Ben's fingers circling her wrist, and the heat of his possession was spreading along every nerve and sinew in her arm. She glanced anxiously about her, but to her relief no one seemed at all interested in what was going on at their table. They might have been alone in the garden.

'And that pleases you, doesn't it?' she retaliated now, realising she would get nowhere by being submissive, but to her annoyance Ben nodded.

'Yes, it pleases me,' he agreed, his gaze dropping insolently down her body. 'It doesn't please me that you chose to keep my son's existence a secret from me, but I remember his conception with rather more accuracy than you do, obviously.'

'Bastard!'

'Liar,' he countered equably. His thumb moved insistently against the network of veins that marked the inner side of her wrist. 'So—what are we going to do?'

Jaime swallowed. 'Don't you mean—what are *you* going to do?'

'No.' Ben's eyes lingered on her mouth. 'I mean, what are *we* going to do. I realise I can't come back after all these years and expect us to take up where we left off——'

'Damn right!'

'But there's still a hell of a lot more than indifference between us, and we both know it.'

'No!' Jaime felt incensed.

'Yes.' Ben was implacable. 'Why do you think I came to find you? I didn't know about Tom then. I didn't know what a consummate little actress you'd turned out to be.'

'If you think——'

'I think we need a lot more time to handle this rationally,' Ben cut in steadily. 'Tom hardly knows me yet. I suggest we let events take their natural course. For the present, anyway.'

Jaime stared at him disbelievingly. 'You can't seriously conceive that I'd let you back into my life!' she exclaimed.

'Do you have a choice?' Ben released her wrist abruptly, and took a mouthful of his beer. Then, wiping the foam from his lip with the back of his hand, he appended, 'I think Tom might have something to say about that.'

Jaime gasped. 'You'd bring Tom into this?'

'Why not?' Ben regarded her without expression. 'He is involved.'

'No.'

'Yes.' Ben lifted his shoulders indifferently. 'I assume you'd rather I didn't tell Phil about him.'

'Phil!' For a few moments, Jaime had forgotten about her ex-husband, but Ben's words struck a chill into her heart. 'That's—that's blackmail,' she said unsteadily.

'No, it's not.' Ben pushed his beer aside. 'I'm not suggesting I would tell Phil. I'm just pointing out the alternatives I have at my disposal.'

Jaime scrubbed at the wrist he had been holding with her other hand, hardly aware of what she was doing. 'If you don't intend telling Phil, then why did you mention him? You're threatening me, Ben. And I despise you for it.'

'You're wrong.' Ben expelled his breath heavily. 'Jaime, all I want is for you to accept the situation as it really is, and not as you'd like to make it.'

Jaime moved her head from side to side. 'And if Tom doesn't want to see you again?'

Ben's mouth flattened. 'He will.'

'Why?' Jaime knew she was losing, but she had to make one final bid for her future. 'Because you can offer him big houses, and big cars, and—and swimming-pools?'

'No.' Ben's response was grim, and when he leaned towards her a *frisson* of fear feathered her spine. 'Believe it or not, I regret what I said on Saturday night,' he told her savagely. 'It was a—gut reaction to your intransigence, but that doesn't alter the fact that I shouldn't have bragged about the house. No, the reason Tom will want to see me again is something much more basic. You may not like it, but we got on rather well. And whatever grudge you think you have against me, I won't let you keep us apart!'

CHAPTER FIVE

THE rest of the week was an anti-climax. Jaime went to work every morning anticipating the worst, and came home every evening fully expecting Ben to have contacted Tom in her absence. But he didn't. Tuesday seeped into Wednesday, and Thursday into Friday, and there was no further communication from him. Indeed, it got to such a point that Jaime actually found herself wondering if he was ill, and although she told herself that that prospect gave her no concern it gave her no satisfaction either. Tom, she knew, was disappointed that his uncle hadn't been in touch. In spite of his brave statement of indifference, he had expected Ben to try to see him again. Of course, he knew nothing about his mother's encounter at the beginning of the week. Jaime had had no choice but to keep that to herself. She only hoped that if Ben did see Tom again he would do the same. She didn't like keeping secrets from her son, but it was too late now to do anything about it.

'Are you going to the disco tonight?' she asked on Friday evening, finding even the prospect of her son's continuing association with Angie Santini preferable to the alternative at the moment, but Tom shook his head.

'No,' he answered. 'I don't feel like it. I think I'll clear out my room instead.'

'Clear out your room?' Jaime turned from straining vegetables at the sink to stare at her son. 'Since when did you clear out your room without being asked?'

'Since now,' exclaimed Tom defensively. 'Well—there's not much else to do, is there?'

Jaime hesitated. 'Well, it's a lovely evening. You could take—Angie—for a walk.'

'Nah.' Tom shook his head again. 'Angie's going to the disco.'

'And you're not?' Jaime couldn't keep the astonishment out of her voice.

'I'm not in the mood,' declared her son, flinging himself into a chair at the table. 'Not tonight, anyway.'

Jaime shook her head now, not quite knowing how to take this unexpected turn of events. She couldn't help thinking that Tom hadn't had these reservations last weekend, and the connection between Ben's visit and her son's sudden aversion to going out was impossible to ignore.

'You've not fallen out with Angie, have you?' she ventured, needing to clarify the situation in her own mind, and Tom looked up at her with guarded eyes.

'No,' he said, toying with the cutlery Jaime had laid on the table. 'Why? Do you want me to go out or something?'

'Of course not.' Jaime was thrown on the defensive now, although another thought had occurred to her. 'It's just not usual for you to spend Friday night at home, that's all. You're not—expecting anyone, are you?'

'Are you?'

'Me?' Jaime was lifting a casserole out of the oven as she spoke, and the word degenerated into a squeak of pain as the dish slipped against her palm. 'Damn,' she added, shoving the offending container on to the hob and pressing her two palms together. 'Who would I be expecting?'

Then, as she was staring somewhat resentfully at her son, the doorbell rang. Like a blatant reaction to her plea of innocence, the sound echoed resonantly around the small kitchen, and Tom was out of his chair and on his way to answer it almost before the chimes died away. But it was the expression he flung at his mother as he did so that caused Jaime's heart to lurch in silent protest. She couldn't be sure, but she thought he believed she knew who it was, and his interpretation was obvious.

Jaime froze as he bounded up the hall, the casserole forgotten on the hob beside her. It had to be Ben, she thought sickly, guessing he had chosen this way to do things to avoid any repetition of the confrontation they had had on Monday. By coming to the house, he was forcing her to accept him. And Tom was simply playing into his hands.

The door opened, but the voice that greeted her son wasn't Ben's. It was female, and as the numbness that had gripped her began to ease Jaime recognised her mother's voice. *Her mother's voice!* A wave of hysteria swept over her, and she had to physically suppress the urge to laugh out loud. It wasn't Ben, it was her mother. Dear God, was she going mad?

'It's Nan,' announced Tom offhandedly, preceding his grandmother into the room, and resuming his seat at the table. He didn't look at his mother, and, conscious of her own weakness, Jaime guessed her son was suffering the same reaction. He had expected it to be Ben, of course, and the sulky twist to his lips was an indication of his disappointment.

'Hi, Mum!'

Jaime greeted her mother warmly, but Mrs Fenner surveyed the pair of them rather wryly. 'Did I interrupt an argument or what?' she asked, setting her handbag down on the floor and unbuttoning her jacket. 'If I'm in the way, I can easily go back home.'

'Don't be silly, Mum.' Jaime flashed her son a reproving look, and went to help her mother off with her coat. 'You're not interrupting anything. We were just going to eat, actually. Why don't you join us?'

'Oh, no.' Mrs Fenner shook her blonde head. Like her daughter—and her grandson—her hair had once been silvery pale, and although its colour now owed more to the skills of her hairdresser than to nature she was still a very attractive woman. 'I'll just make myself a cup of tea, if that's all right with you. It's so hot! It's years since we've had a summer like this.'

'Are you sure you won't have something to eat?' Jaime moved the casserole on to the table, and took off the lid. 'It's your favourite—chicken.'

'Honestly.' Her mother fanned herself with a languid hand. 'Besides, I had a sandwich before I came out. And I mustn't stay long. I promised your father I'd be back before the place got busy.'

'All right.' Jaime looked at her son again. 'Why don't you fill the kettle, Tom?'

'Oh, sure——'

Tom would have got up from the table there and then, but his grandmother's hand kept him in his chair. 'Stay where you are!' she exclaimed, patting his shoulder. 'When the day comes that I can't fill a kettle for myself, I'll let you know.'

Jaime sighed but, setting the plates on the table, she took her seat. She noticed that Tom avoided her eyes as she ladled some of the delicious-smelling casserole on to his plate, and she guessed he was having a hard time hiding his feelings. She couldn't help wondering what she would have done if it had been Ben at the door. From now on, that would always be a possibility, and it wasn't easy to come to terms with.

'So, to what do we owe the honour of this visit?' she asked now, making a determined effort to act naturally. 'Dad's OK, isn't he? There's nothing wrong?'

'Heavens, no!'

But her mother's response was almost too prompt, and Jaime was disturbed. It was rare that her mother came here unannounced, and never at this time of day. There had to be a reason. But what?

'I—er—I've been to the Cash and Carry,' Mrs Fenner said quickly, putting two tea-bags into the pot. 'I just thought I'd call in—as you didn't come over last weekend.'

'Oh.' That sounded reasonable, but after handing Tom his plate Jaime made no attempt to fill her own. 'Well— as you know, it was the Haines's party on Saturday night, and we just had a lazy day on Sunday.'

'Late night, huh?' suggested her mother mildly, and Jaime wondered what all this was really about.

'Not really——' she was beginning slowly, when Tom broke in.

'Uncle Ben came here last Saturday night,' he interjected, ignoring his mother's sudden intake of breath. 'He came while Mum was out. But he stayed until she got home.'

'Did he?' Now it was Mrs Fenner's turn to look disturbed, and she turned half anxious, half accusing eyes in her daughter's direction. 'You never said.'

'Well—I haven't had the chance, have I?' Jaime knew she had no need to feel guilty, but she did. 'I—would have——'

'So, he spent the evening with Tom,' Mrs Fenner murmured faintly, and her grandson nodded.

'Yes. And he was really nice,' he declared, through a mouthful of chicken and vegetables. 'He told me all about working for the BBC, and what it was like living in South Africa. His wife died out there, you know. Auntie Maura, that is. Apparently, she'd been ill for years.' He paused, and looked defensively at his mother. 'Did you know that, Mum?'

Jaime got up from the table. 'I've told you, Tom, I've got no interest in anything Ben Russell says or does. Now—can we change the subject? Mum——' she looked to her mother for assistance '—why don't you go and sit outside? I'll bring a tray out to you.'

'Oh—very well.'

Mrs Fenner looked as if she would have liked to argue, but discretion, and her daughter's tense face, persuaded her otherwise. With a rueful smile at Tom, she opened the back door and stepped out on to the sunny patio.

'I suppose you think I shouldn't have told Nan,' Tom muttered in a low voice as soon as his grandmother was out of earshot, but Jaime only shook her head.

'It doesn't matter to me who you tell,' she retorted, though the cups and saucers clattered a bit as she set them on the tray. 'Finish your meal. There's seconds if you want them.'

It was a relief to step outside. At this hour of the afternoon the sun's rays were muted by the fronds of the willow tree that trailed in a corner of the garden. There were stripes of sun and shadow across the wrought-iron table, where Jaime set the tray, and the warm air was scented with the perfume of the flowers.

Jaime pushed the tray towards her mother, and then flopped into the chair opposite. But if she had hoped that by escaping from the house she had escaped thinking about Ben Russell she was mistaken.

'Does he know?'

The question was oblique, but Jaime knew exactly what it meant. 'He thinks he does.'

'What does that mean?' Mrs Fenner stared at her daughter with wide eyes. 'Did you tell him?'

'I didn't have to,' replied Jaime wearily. 'He'd seen Tom. He guessed.'

'But—Tom doesn't look like the Russells.'

'Apparently, he does. Ben's father, anyway. Besides, when you see them together, the likeness is unmistakable. It's not so much in appearance. It's more to do with their personality, their character.'

'Well, I hope Tom doesn't have his father's weaknesses!' exclaimed Mrs Fenner shortly. 'Honestly, Jaime, I thought all that was behind us!'

'Do you think I didn't?'

There was a suspicious brightness to Jaime's eyes as she looked at her mother, and Mrs Fenner clicked her tongue in sympathy. 'You should have rung and told us. I wondered why I hadn't heard from you.'

Jaime sniffed, and determinedly straightened her spine. 'Is that why you came?'

'No.' Mrs Fenner pulled a rueful face as she poured two cups of tea, and passed one over to her daughter. 'Actually——' She glanced towards the house to assure herself that Tom wasn't eavesdropping on their conversation, and then continued, 'Actually, I came to warn you, that—that *he'd* moved into the Priory.'

'Oh, I see.' Jaime heaved a sigh, and took a determined mouthful of her tea. 'And Tom stole your thunder.'

'Well, it wasn't quite like that,' retorted her mother drily. 'Although, I must admit, I'm disappointed that you didn't feel we had a right to know what was happening. For heaven's sake, Jaime, this could cause all sorts of complications.'

'I know.'

'I gather he didn't tell Tom.'

Jaime put down her cup. 'No.'

'And you haven't?'

Jaime made a sound of impatience. 'Is that likely?'

Mrs Fenner bit her lip. 'Well, what's he going to do?'

'I don't know.' Jaime felt desperate, and sounded it. 'He—he suggests we just—play it by ear.'

Mrs Fenner blinked. 'Well, I must say he's taking it rather coolly, isn't he? I don't know that I'd have his presence of mind.'

Jaime shrugged. 'The Russells aren't like us, are they?'

'Even so...' Her mother frowned. 'I gather you managed to speak to him alone.'

'Well—yes.' Jaime shifted a little uncomfortably. 'I—I had lunch with him on Monday.'

'You've been out with him!'

Her mother sounded quite scandalised now, and Jaime hurried to reassure her. 'It wasn't my idea. He came to the office. On Monday lunchtime,' she explained. 'Obviously, he couldn't say anything while—while Tom was around, and—well, I didn't have a lot of choice in the matter.'

'It didn't occur to him that Tom might be Philip's son, not his?' her mother queried doubtfully, and Jaime uttered a tired sigh.

'Yes,' she said, resting her elbows on the table, closing her eyes and sliding slim fingers into the damp hair at her temples. 'Of course, that was what he thought at first.'

'But you disabused him?'

'No, Mum. He guessed. I told you.' Jaime's head was beginning to throb, and she felt that if she heard one more word about Ben Russell she'd scream. She opened her eyes again, and looked hollowly at her mother. 'Now, can we talk about something else?'

Mrs Fenner frowned. 'You can't expect me not to be curious, Jaime. For heaven's sake, the man comes back to Kingsmere, after all these years, and the first person he comes to see is you!' She paused. 'You must admit, it was a coincidence.'

'It's not a coincidence at all.' Jaime looked away towards the roses, which were espaliered against the wall that divided her garden from the one next door. 'He'd heard I was living here. I suppose he thought it was only polite to make contact.'

'Rubbish!' Mrs Fenner spoke disparagingly. 'If your relationship with that man had been a normal one, I might have believed you. But after what he did to you——'

'Oh, Mum, shut up, will you?' Jaime didn't think she could take any more, and she cast an anxious glance at the open kitchen door. 'Don't you think I have enough to worry about?' she exclaimed, her eyes darting pointedly towards the house. 'I don't need you to tell me what I already know.'

'Well, I'm sorry.' Her mother shrugged somewhat huffily. 'But I worry about you, Jaime. And I wonder what he'll do, that's all. I mean, he's not well, is he?'

Jaime's drifting attention focused on her mother's face. 'Not well?'

'No. That's why he came back to England, isn't it? For treatment. Didn't you know?'

Jaime tried to remember what Tom had told her. He had said that Ben had been ill, and that that was why he had come back to England. But she hadn't paid much attention to Tom's explanations, deciding they had been offered as a sop to Tom's pride rather than a true representation of the facts. Oh, she had seen for herself how Ben had changed, and she was quite prepared to accept that living in a war zone must be tough, but she had not allowed herself to feel any sympathy for him. Now, however...

'You didn't know?' Mrs Fenner sounded surprised. 'Well, it seems my journey hasn't been entirely wasted. Yes, according to what I've heard he has some kind of liver problem.'

Jaime's stomach heaved, and she got abruptly to her feet. A liver problem! she thought sickly. Oh, God! Liver problems could be terminal, couldn't they? Surely that wasn't why he had come back to England—*to die?*

'Where are you going?'

Her mother's voice reaching her from across the courtyard made Jaime realise she had started almost involuntarily towards the house, and she came to an uncertain stop. But her initial instincts had been to find out if it was true, by whatever means she had at her disposal.

'Oh—I was just going to see if Tom had finished his meal,' she offered lamely, but she could tell from her mother's expression that she was not deceived.

'You can't still care about him,' Mrs Fenner whispered disbelievingly, and although her words were barely audible Jaime couldn't pretend she hadn't heard them.

'*No!*' she responded fiercely. 'No, of course I don't care about him. But—God! You can't tell me something like that without producing some reaction.' She ran a dazed hand over her forehead. 'Who told you?'

Mrs Fenner sighed. 'Oh—I don't remember now. You know how these things get about. People will talk, and pubs are veritable hotbeds of gossip.'

'Is it serious?' Jaime had to know.

'I don't know.' Her mother got to her feet now. 'Look, I've got to go. I've already stayed longer than I intended, and your father has his Chamber of Trade meeting tonight.'

'Of course.' Jaime nodded. 'Um—give Dad our love, won't you?'

'Will you be all right?' Mrs Fenner stopped beside her daughter, and put a worried hand on Jaime's shoulder. 'I didn't mean to upset you. I just thought you ought to know, that's all.'

'It's OK, Mum. Honestly.'

Somehow, Jaime managed to reassure her that she was fine, and Tom's presence prevented any further confidences. Besides, what else was there to say? thought Jaime, as she waved her mother away. Just because Ben had apparently contracted some kind of tropical complaint did not mean he was dying. She was over-reacting. He'd said he'd picked up a bug in Africa, and that was a far cry from liver failure, which was what she had first thought of. No, he would survive. The problem was, would she?

CHAPTER SIX

THE weekend dragged by. Jaime refused to accept that both she and Tom were suffering the effects of Ben's failure to get in touch, but the fact remained that they each, for their own reasons, had expected that he would.

For Jaime's part, she blamed Tom for creating such an air of gloom and despondency about the place. He wouldn't contact his friends; he wouldn't go out. He just lounged in front of the television set, switching channels, and generally making a nuisance of himself.

Which wasn't like him, she thought frustratedly. Until Ben Russell had come on the scene, Tom had been a fairly well-balanced teenager and, in retrospect, even his infatuation for Angie Santini seemed completely natural. And he and she had always got along so well together. In fact, she used to feel rather smug, when the other women at work had complained about their children. She had had no real problems with Tom. Until now.

Damn Ben Russell, she thought on Sunday evening, as she prepared for bed. It was typical of him to dangle the prospect of his exciting life under Tom's nose, and then withdraw it again, untried. Was that how he was going to get his revenge against her? By hurting his own son?

Monday was a hectic day, and by mid-afternoon Jaime's head was aching badly. It felt like the start of a migraine, and as Felix had appointments all afternoon she rang him and asked if he'd mind if she left early.

'Would you like someone to drive you home?' he asked, after giving her his blessing, and Jaime thought how considerate some men were compared to others.

'No, I can manage,' she demurred, wanting only to be on her own for a while. 'But thanks, anyway. I'll see you in the morning.'

The house was hot, after being shut up all day, and she opened all the windows, and the back door, before settling down with a cup of tea and two aspirins. It was only three o'clock. Tom wouldn't be home for another hour yet. She could relax.

A fly came in the door and began buzzing at the window, and Jaime sighed. Flies were such stupid creatures, she thought irritably. No sooner did they get into the house than they were trying to get out again. And how was it they could find the doorway perfectly easily coming in, but completely lost direction afterwards?

The window was open, too, so all the thing had to do was circle to the right to get out. But, of course, it didn't. It just kept on buzzing around in the middle of the pane, until the tension it was creating forced Jaime to get up again to dispose of it. And, as she was endeavouring to sweep it to freedom, the phone rang.

'Oh, great!' Jaime cast one last malevolent look at the insect, and then, throwing down the newspaper she had been using as a tool, she stalked into the hall, and snatched up the receiver. 'Yes?'

The voice was unmistakable. It had haunted her dreams for the last ten days and, although she had no desire to speak to him, she couldn't help the involuntary response of her body.

'Ben.' She didn't pretend not to recognise him. But her tone was distant—in direct contradiction to her emotions. 'What do you want?'

'I thought you might be interested to know that Tom's here,' declared Ben flatly. 'Do you want to speak to him?'

Jaime wanted to sit down, but she didn't. Instead, she hung on to the phone as if it might offer some remnant of support. 'Tom's—there!'

Ben expelled his breath. 'Yes.'

'Oh, God!' Jaime caught her breath. 'What have you done?'

'*I* haven't done anything,' retorted Ben smoothly. 'As I say, I think you should speak to Tom.'

'Did you go to his school?' Jaime was beside herself. 'Did you bribe him with promises of lunch? I suppose you realised you were wasting your time with me, so you decided to use Tom——'

But she was speaking to herself. The phone had been laid down, and she could hear the sound of footsteps on an uncarpeted floor. Then she heard a muffled exchange, and other footsteps, lighter ones this time, before the phone was picked up once more.

'Mum?'

'Tom!' Jaime could barely articulate his name. She swallowed convulsively. 'Tom, what are you doing there?'

'Oh, Mum.' Tom sounded sheepish, and Jaime's nerves tightened. What did Tom have to be sheepish about? He couldn't help being attracted by so much wealth. 'Mum, I'm sorry.'

Jaime drew a steadying breath. 'There's no need to be sorry, Tom,' she said evenly. 'Naturally, I'm disappointed that you've missed an afternoon's school. Still, it's only half a day. I dare say you can make it up tomorrow.'

'You don't mind my coming here, then?' Tom was obviously anxious, and Jaime was reassured. So long as Tom cared about her feelings, she had nothing to worry about.

'Well,' she murmured now, wondering whether Ben was eavesdropping on their conversation, 'I don't suppose you could refuse. Did—er—did Uncle Ben meet you from school?'

'No.' Tom sounded puzzled now. 'No, he didn't even know I was coming, did he?'

Didn't he?

Jaime had to sit down then. She groped her way to the foot of the stairs, and sank down weakly on to one of the lower treads. What was Tom saying? That he had gone to Ben's house uninvited?

'I—I think you'd better explain what happened,' she managed, after a few moments. 'Are you saying that you—that *you* decided to play truant?'

'Kids don't play truant these days, Mum,' muttered Tom, a little sulkily. 'They skive off—or they split!'

'Thank you. But I don't require a lesson in semantics, Tom,' retorted Jaime shortly, and as a justifiable anger began to replace the panic inside her she added, 'How dare you go there without my permission?'

Tom sniffed. 'It wasn't like that.'

'What do you mean, it wasn't like that? You've just told me you—you abandoned school, and that—that Uncle Ben wasn't expecting you.'

'I know.' Tom's reply was defensive. 'But I didn't intend to come to the house. I—just wanted to see where it was, that's all.'

Jaime breathed deeply. 'So? What happened?'

'Uncle Ben saw me.'

'He saw you?'

'Yes.' Tom hesitated. 'He—I—I was outside the gates, when he drove in.'

'I see.' Jaime tried to keep a lid on her temper. 'And he recognised you, of course.'

'Well—I waved,' muttered Tom lamely, and Jaime closed her eyes against the visions that his words evoked. Ben turning into the gates of the Priory, and Tom trying madly to attract his attention. God! And she had virtually accused Ben of kidnapping! No wonder he had put the phone down on her.

'I think you'd better put—Uncle Ben back on the phone,' Jaime declared now, steeling herself for another confrontation. 'And I think you should come home. Right away.'

'Oh, Mum!'

'Just put Ben—*Uncle* Ben back on, will you? Anything I have to say to you can wait until you get home.'

'But I want to go swimming!'

'Not today, Tom. Now, let me speak to—to your uncle.'

Once again, the phone was laid down, this time rather less considerately, and she heard the exchange of feet on the bare floor. Tiles? she wondered inconsequentially, and then dashed the insidious thought. She had absolutely no interest in how Ben Russell had restored the Priory. She was only concerned with its occupant, and the effect he was having on her family.

The phone was lifted, and once again Ben came on the line. 'Washed your mouth out with soap?' he queried laconically, and Jaime was so relieved he wasn't angry with her that a nervous laugh escaped her.

'I'm sorry.'

'No problem.' Ben was unperturbed. 'I just thought you might get worried if he didn't arrive home from school at the usual time.'

'Well, I would have, of course.' Jaime had her incipient hysteria under control now, and she was able to think of other things. 'How—how did you know I was here?'

'I looked in my crystal ball.' Ben's tone was dry. 'How do you think? I phoned your office, and the receptionist told me you'd gone home. She said you weren't feeling well. Are you all right?'

'Oh—yes.' Jaime wasn't concerned about her own condition right now. With luck, the receptionist wouldn't have asked who he was, so Felix was unlikely to hear about it. 'Um—I'm sorry if Tom's disrupted your afternoon. I had no idea he might—well, I'll speak to him myself, when he gets home.'

'As I say, it's no problem.' Ben was infuriatingly casual. 'He was curious to see where I lived. I can understand that.'

Yes, you would! thought Jaime tautly, willing herself not to say anything that might jeopardise her chances of getting Tom home again unscathed. At least, now, she had some idea of what she was up against, so far as her son was concerned. Whatever he said, Tom wasn't going to ignore his relationship to the Russells. That was blatantly obvious.

'Well, I think you'd better send him home—right away,' she declared now, trying hard to sound reasonable. 'The—the bus from Nettleford to Kingsmere passes close to the Priory gates. He can get that. He does have some money with him.'

'OK. If that's what you want.' If she'd expected an argument from Ben, she was disappointed. 'I can think of an alternative, but you're his mother.'

'Yes, I am.' Jaime's response came out curter than she could have wished, but she couldn't help it. She licked her lips. 'Tell—tell Tom I'll pick him up at the bus station.'

There was a moment's pause, and then Ben said quietly, 'Why don't you come and get him yourself?'

His suggestion was delivered in the same even tone he had used before, and Jaime envied him his ability to

hide his feelings so well. For her part, she was left scrab-
bling for a legitimate excuse.

'I—don't think so,' she said at last, not very satisfactorily, and Ben sighed.

'All right.' As before, he didn't attempt to try to
change her mind. 'I'll give Tom your message——'

'Wait!'

Jaime realised he intended to ring off, and all of a
sudden she was aware of how skilfully he had transferred the responsibility for what happened next to her.
He could tell Tom—quite truthfully—that his mother
had insisted he go home, and, remembering her son's
attitude over the past weekend, Jaime could imagine how
that would be received. It might be what she wanted,
but was it really wise to play into Ben's hands by acting
the heavy?

'I—uh—what was your alternative?' she enquired,
through clenched teeth, and had the dubious pleasure
of knowing she had disconcerted him for once.

But Ben was nothing if not resourceful, and he quickly
regained his composure. 'I was going to offer to bring
him home myself—later,' he appended smoothly. 'After
he's had time to look around—and take a swim.'

'He doesn't have his swimming shorts,' Jaime protested at once. It was the first thing that came into her
head, but Ben was undeterred.

'There's only the two of us here, and we're both male,'
he reminded her mildly. 'But, if he's shy, he can borrow
a pair of mine. We can fix something.'

'I'm sure.'

Jaime was terse, but she couldn't help it. The idea of
her son being rewarded for ducking out of school, and
visiting the Priory without telling her first, rankled. Even
without the very real threat Ben presented in all this. He
was forcing her to trust him, and it wasn't easy. The
truth was, images of Ben and Tom swimming together
caused other, equally disturbing reactions. Not least,
images of Ben as she had once seen him, and the devastating effect he had had on her life.

'You're not happy?'

Ben was asking the question, and Jaime struggled to
recover a sense of proportion. 'I—don't know what to

say,' she admitted honestly, incapable in that moment of prevaricating. 'Oh—all right. He can stay. For an hour, at least. I'll meet him at the bus station at a quarter to five.'

She thought Ben might have insisted that he would bring Tom home, but he didn't. Instead, he accepted her terms without debate, and before Jaime could say anything more he rang off. He's probably disappointed because he's got nothing to blame me for, she decided defiantly, but her ebullience was short-lived. Ben still had Tom—and more than an hour to poison the boy's mind against her.

It was impossible to relax after that. Jaime finished her tea, and washed up the cups, but she found herself consulting her watch every few minutes. However, nothing could accelerate the passage of time, and after turning the television on and then off again in quick succession she went upstairs to have a wash and renew her make-up.

Her reflection in the mirror above the hand-basin was not reassuring. She looked harassed and drawn, she thought bitterly. It was just as well her hair was that silvery shade of blonde. She was sure she must have acquired a great many grey hairs since she had learned Ben was coming to live in Kingsmere, but at least they didn't show. Nevertheless, the strain on her nerves was undeniable, and she tipped her head back on her shoulders as exhaustion took its toll.

Still, a few moments later the skilful application of cosmetics had removed much of the evidence. The shadows around her eyes had disappeared beneath a dusky powder, and a creamy blusher had added colour to her pale cheeks. With the generous contours of her mouth outlined by a tawny lip-gloss, she was moderately pleased with the results. She might still be able to see her anxiety, but she was sure that Tom would not.

She changed from the shirt dress she had worn to the office into a pair of loose-fitting cotton trousers and a sleeveless vest. Because they were white, they accentuated the slight tan she had acquired during the hours she had spent in the garden and, like the make-up, they were a determined attempt to lift her spirits. Superficially, she looked good, she decided firmly. Good enough to convince Tom she wasn't beaten yet.

It was still too early to go and meet him, however. Although Kingsmere was a small town, it did have its rush-hour, and Jaime had no intention of trying to find anywhere to park near the bus station. She planned to wait until Tom had had time to get outside the terminal. That way she hoped to be able to pick him up without having to park at all.

She was standing in the living-room, gazing impatiently out of the window, when the sleek Mercedes glided to a halt behind her small Renault. It was barely four-thirty, and she hadn't even thought about leaving yet. She had estimated it would take her ten minutes at most to reach the town centre. And Ben must have known that, she hazarded. How she wished she had left early. It was galling being so predictable.

Even so, she couldn't prevent the shiver of apprehension that shivered down her spine as Ben turned off the ignition, and got out of the vehicle. Tom was getting out, too, hauling his school haversack off the back seat, and looking not a little apprehensive himself now that the excitement was over and he had to face his mother.

She had to go to the door, Jaime knew that. She had to open the door, and behave as if nothing monumental had happened, not least because she knew the car's arrival would have caused quite a stir in the neighbourhood. There was no way she could grab Tom and drag him inside without creating a disturbance, but the very idea of being civil, when she felt so *angry*, almost choked her.

Tom was first up the steps, his guarded expression revealing his awareness of the enormity of what he had done. It was the first time he had done anything without clearing it with his mother first, and Jaime guessed he wasn't as confident as he would like her to think. He didn't know how she was going to react, and he wasn't yet old enough not to care.

His hair was wet, Jaime noticed, and, looking beyond her son to the man who had followed him through the garden gate, she saw that Ben's hair was damp, too. So

Tom had had his swim, she thought painfully, realising that the small betrayal hurt more than anything.

'Uncle Ben said that, as you weren't feeling well, he'd bring me home,' Tom volunteered now, brushing past his mother and into the hall of the house. He glanced at her defiantly. 'I must say, you look OK to me.'

'Do I?' Jaime managed the flat rejoinder, and then steeled herself to turn back to Ben. 'How kind of you to think of me!'

'You don't think so,' observed Ben, halting on the flagged path below her. 'Do you?'

Jaime stifled the desire to agree with him, and lifted her shoulders. 'It's not important. Tom's home now. I'm grateful.'

Ben tossed his car keys and caught them, and then thrust his hands into the pockets of his trousers. He was wearing black denims and a beige silk shirt, which accentuated the darkness of his skin. But for all that, he still had a look of fatigue around his eyes, and Jaime found herself remembering what her mother had said.

'Right,' he said at last. 'I'll be in touch.'

Tom came forward. 'Aren't you coming in?'

Ben's mouth twisted. 'I don't think so.' His gaze shifted to Jaime. 'I don't think your mother wants company right now.'

'Mum?'

Tom was still looking frustratedly at her when they all heard the sound of running footsteps coming down the street. Dragging her gaze away from her son's, Jaime turned her head to see who it was, and then felt an overwhelming sense of relief when Angie Santini stopped at the gate.

'Tom!' Angie exclaimed, sweeping back the tumbled weight of her hair with a knowingly sensual hand. 'Where've you been? I've been waiting outside the lab for ages!'

Tom coloured and, evidently satisfied with this result, Angie came through the gate. But her attention had moved to the other male present, and Jaime's feelings did a quick about-face as the girl's eyes lingered on Ben. She gave his leanly muscled frame a thorough appraisal, and then glanced meaningfully over her shoulder at the Mercedes parked outside.

'Nice car!' she murmured, a knowing smile lifting the corners of her lips, and Tom squeezed past his mother again to make the introduction.

'It's my uncle's,' he said proudly, and Jaime's fists clenched as she turned back into the house.

She was in the kitchen, pulling saucepans out of the cupboard, when she became aware that she was no longer alone. Red-faced from her exertions, she turned, expecting to find Tom and Angie behind her. But it wasn't her son and his girlfriend. It was Ben standing in the open doorway, and her feelings coalesced into a burning resentment.

'I thought you were leaving!' she exclaimed, slamming a saucepan down on to the drainer, and Ben took a deep breath before walking into the room.

'I think you should calm down,' he said, as she turned to face him. 'You're going to give yourself a heart attack if you go on like this.'

'What would you know about it?' Jaime's hand itched to slap his impassive face. 'You come here and seduce my son with expensive toys, and expect me to be happy about it!'

'He's my son, too,' replied Ben, in a low, forceful voice, and Jaime caught her breath. But when her eyes darted anxiously past his shoulder, Ben raised a soothing hand. 'It's all right,' he said. 'Tom's outside with—Angie, is it? I'd say he has his hands full for now.'

'Well, Angie is quite a handful, as I'm sure you've noticed,' muttered Jaime, turning back to the sink, and then stiffened when Ben moved to rest his hands on the drainer at either side of her.

'You wouldn't be jealous, by any chance?' he murmured, his breath lifting the hair at the nape of her neck, and Jaime lifted a hand to protect the vulnerable flesh.

'Don't—don't be silly,' she snapped, but she didn't trust herself to turn towards him. She was too intensely conscious of the heat of his body behind her, and the faint smell of him, that mingled shaving soap and deodorant, and the musky male scent of his skin.

'You don't have to be,' he continued, and she wondered if he was aware of the effect he was having on her weakened senses. His lips grazed the skin of her knuckles, and she withdrew her hand abruptly, only to regret having done so when his mouth touched the sensitive curve of her nape. 'Compared to Angie, you're as ripe and luscious as a peach.'

'Fat and overblown, is that what you mean?' retorted Jaime witheringly, desperate to dispel the disturbing intimacy of his words, but Ben was not deterred.

'You're not fat, and you know it,' he said, stepping closer, and Jaime had to press her stomach against the sink to avoid brushing against him. 'You were never thin. That was one of the things I liked about you. You hadn't sacrificed shape for style.'

'Un—unlike—Maura,' Jaime choked, hoping the mention of his dead wife's name would bring him to his senses. But it didn't.

Instead of moving away, his mouth sought the skin at the side of her neck, and although she jerked her head away he bit into the soft flesh. 'Don't expect me to make comparisons,' he said, one hand leaving the unit to curve possessively over her hip. 'You were the only woman I loved. Let that be enough for you.'

'You can't say that——'

'I just did.'

'You never loved me——'

'What would you know about it?'

He used both hands then to turn her resisting body to face him, and, although she strained away from him, his hands on her hips made her increasingly aware of his arousal.

'Ben,' she began, hoping to reason with him, but something—some frustrated need, perhaps—was fighting her resistance. She wanted to push him away from her. She wanted to escape from the sensual strength of his hands, and rekindle the hatred she knew she should be feeling towards him, but she couldn't. She didn't know why. Maybe it was their unfamiliar isolation—the realisation that for the first time since Ben had come back into her life they were really alone. There were no people around them here. No fellow diners at the pub by the river, no Tom in the next room, straining to hear every word they said. Oh, Tom wasn't far away. Jaime thought she could hear his and Angie's voices mingling in the garden outside. But, for the moment, they were absorbed with their own affairs. Not with hers.

Ben was looking at her. She could see the darkening heat of passion in his green eyes, and her knees trembled. His lips were slightly parted and the warmth of his breath was fanning her temple. She could feel his awareness, sense his hunger. The throbbing power in his loins was melting every bone in her body, and when he bent his head towards her she didn't have the will to fight him.

His lips were hot and sensuous, yet, for all that, she sensed the restraint he was putting on himself. She guessed he was aware that if Tom should come and find them in such a compromising position he might ask questions Ben was not prepared to answer. But he couldn't disguise his need. Between ragged gulps of air he savaged any protest she might have tried to make, and as her opposition waned his tongue plunged urgently into her mouth.

Reality slipped—for both of them. When Ben's hands moved over her hips and drew her even closer to his taut body, Jaime could only clutch at his shoulders. Her head was swimming, and the consuming desire Ben was communicating narrowed her world to one of needs and sensations. Sanity deserted her entirely when he caressed her buttocks, and when his fingers probed the sensitive cleft between, and used it to part her legs, his thigh riding between them became a vital support.

The blood was pounding in her ears now, deafening her to anything but what was going on in this room. Her fingers encountered the open neck of his shirt, and the warm column of his throat was an irresistible temptation. Almost instinctively, her nails disposed of the buttons at the top of his shirt, and when he released her mouth to take a shuddering breath she pressed her lips to his chest.

His groan was barely audible, but she felt its vibration against her tongue. She guessed he was on the brink of losing all control, and the knowledge of the power she now had over him was a tantalising discovery. The in—

timacy of their embrace, the speed with which it had developed, and the desperate way he sought her mouth again revealed his weakness. Nevertheless, when he drew her tongue between his lips and suckled on its tip, she was left in no doubt as to her own weaknesses. She wanted this, just as much as he did, and any thought of capitalising on her advantage was lost...

CHAPTER SEVEN

JAIME wondered later what might have happened if Tom
hadn't interrupted them. Although the idea of Ben taking
her against the kitchen unit might sound incredible—
unbelievable—in retrospect, the fact was they had both
been beyond the point of caring what was proper and
what was not. The fine veneer of civilisation had been
swept away, and its place had been taken by raw,
primitive passion.

But some sixth sense seemed to warn Ben of the
moment when Tom decided to come and find out what
was going on. In less charitable moments, Jaime would
wonder if it weren't a sixth sense honed by years of living
on his wits, but at the time she was just grateful for his
quick thinking. Without the speed of his reactions, Tom
would have surprised them in what could at the very
least be described as embarrassing circumstances, and
the thought of having to face her son in such circumstances, after what she had said about Ben, was
unthinkable.

As it was, she was still struggling to regain her composure when Tom appeared in the kitchen doorway. The
fact that Ben had put the width of the room between
them before her son could suspect their behaviour was
really not enough. Jaime was still reeling from the effects of Ben's lovemaking, and, although she strove to
suppress it, part of her ached from the suddenness of
his withdrawal. She noticed that, although Ben appeared to have regained control of his senses, he had
dragged his shirt out of his trousers, and thrust his hands
into his pockets. The realisation of why he had done so
hit Jaime with some force, and a guilty wave of colour
stained cheeks that were already burning.

'Hey...' Tom's gaze flicked between them with some
concern and, for a second, Jaime thought he had guessed

what had occurred. But, happily, her son was still too young to jump to what Jaime believed was a fairly obvious conclusion. Because he had never been exposed to a normal family relationship, Tom still regarded sex as something his generation had discovered, and the idea that his mother might succumb to uncontrollable impulses simply didn't occur to him. 'Have you two been fighting over me?'

Jaime heard the breath Ben expelled, and then he straightened his spine with a definite effort. 'We've been—exploring—possibilities,' he said, and only Jaime understood the real significance of that remark. 'Nothing for you to worry about.'

'Is that right?' Tom turned to his mother. 'Is it?'

Jaime ran her damp palms over her cheeks. She had to get control of herself, she told herself severely. But her brain felt scrambled, and it was difficult to even formulate a coherent response.

'I—yes,' she got out at last. It was letting Tom off the hook, she knew, but just at present she wasn't in a fit state to take him on.

'You mean, you've sorted things out? About my going to see Uncle Ben?' Tom could hardly believe his luck. 'Hey, magic!'

Jaime checked the hair at her nape, and then allowed her hands to slide down the sides of her breasts. It was only when she saw Ben watching her that she realised her actions could be regarded as provocative, and as she twisted her hands together at her waist she realised her body was as shameless as his. But, unlike him, there was no way she could hide the evidence.

'I—think what your mother's saying is that she's forgiven you this time,' Ben declared, his gaze shifting abruptly to the boy. 'That's not to say you should do such a thing again. Not without asking her first, I mean. But I think your mother and I understand one another better now.'

Do we?

Jaime was tempted to dispute that. As her brain cleared, and sanity returned, all the old fears and resentments she had felt towards Ben were rekindled. How dared he stand there and presume to tell Tom what she was thinking? Did he see what had happened as proof of the power he still had over her? Didn't he realise she could only despise him for taking advantage of her—*again*? Just because he had proved she was sexually vulnerable didn't mean he could manipulate her at will.

'Where's Angie?' she asked, deciding she couldn't deal with that right now, and the crispness of her tone was obviously a surprise to both of them.

'Um—she's gone home,' Tom murmured, the confidence he had shown a few minutes earlier withering in the coolness of her appraisal. 'Is—er—is Uncle Ben staying for dinner?'

You wish! thought Jaime bitterly, but she managed to contain her contempt. 'Not tonight,' she replied smoothly, allowing Ben to take that any way he wished. 'Perhaps you'd like to see him to the door? He was just leaving.'

Tom's jaw clenched. 'Does he have to?'

'Yes, he does,' Jaime was beginning irritably, when Ben himself came to her aid.

'Yes, I do,' he confirmed, tucking his shirt back into his waistband with an enviable lack of self-consciousness. 'As a matter of fact, I've got some people coming to supper this evening, and it wouldn't do if the host had already eaten, would it?'

His attempt at humour didn't really mollify Tom, however, and although she hadn't thought about it earlier Jaime couldn't help noticing that Ben was looking distinctly strained. Her mother shouldn't have repeated the gossip about him, she fretted impatiently. Ben wouldn't like to think people were talking about him, she was sure of that, and, for all his faults, she had never known him to show any serious concern for his health. So why should she?

Nevertheless, the curtness of her farewell was as much an acknowledgement of the unwelcome anxieties he aroused inside her as an indication of her mood. She was uncomfortably aware that she hadn't even asked him how he was, and even if she told herself she didn't care she knew she really did. It was a frustrating anomaly that she could hate him for the way he had treated her, and yet still worry about some probably exaggerated complaint he was supposed to be suffering.

As Tom saw him to the door, Jaime pretended to be too busy to accompany them. She didn't need to hear the proprietorial note in Ben's voice to know that she hadn't seen the last of him. He would be back, and there was absolutely nothing she could do about it.

Unwillingly, she found herself wondering who he had invited to supper at the Priory. She wouldn't have been human if she hadn't felt some curiosity about his visitors, and she was aware that the prospect that at least half of them would be female nibbled away at her fragile composure. She didn't care that they were *women*, she told herself crossly. What had happened between her and Ben this afternoon had proved to her, once and for all, that he was totally unscrupulous, totally selfish. And here she was, worrying about his health, while he did his best to ruin it.

Tom's return thankfully curtailed thoughts of that sort, but his expression was not encouraging. He stood, leaning against the door-frame, with a definite look of resentment on his thin, good-looking face. Jaime surmised he was wondering how she was going to respond, now that he didn't have Ben to back him up, but in this— as in so many things, she thought laconically—she was wrong.

'What happened?' he asked, after a few seconds, and Jaime's brows ascended in sudden surprise.

'I beg your pardon?'

'Between you and Uncle Ben?' said Tom offhandedly. 'He—he didn't—hurt you, did he?'

'Hurt me?'

Jaime was glad she had taken the potatoes out of the cupboard in his absence, and was consequently able to concentrate on the task of scraping them instead of holding her son's troubled gaze.

'Yes.' Tom pushed himself away from the door, and came further into the room. 'The way you said he did before.'

'I——' Jaime swallowed. 'When did I say that?'

'Well, you said he assaulted you once,' Tom reminded her gruffly. 'And when I came in just now it was obvious something had been happening.'

Jaime sighed, feeling a rising sense of indignation as she did so. Why couldn't Tom have voiced these deductions while Ben was here to deal with them? she wondered exasperatedly. Why couldn't he have put his 'uncle' on the spot, and not her?

'All right,' she said, attacking the potato in her hand with unmerited savagery, 'we did—have words.' *Words!* 'What did you expect?'

Tom hunched his shoulders and pushed his hands into his pockets. 'You really don't like Uncle Ben, do you?' he muttered. 'I don't know why. It wasn't his fault that Dad walked out on us.'

'No.' Jaime dropped the mutilated potato into the water, and groped about for another. 'And I'm not saying you shouldn't see him again. Just—don't expect me to encourage you.'

Naturally, that wasn't the end of it. Although Tom wasn't happy with Jaime's attitude, he was still too young to hide his feelings. The events of the afternoon had been too exciting to ignore, and in spite of her feelings he spent a good part of the evening that followed describing what he had seen and what he had done.

Jaime told herself she wasn't interested in the renovations Ben had made to the Priory, that Tom's descriptions of large rooms, opening one from another, meant nothing to her. But she couldn't close her mind to his words. The images they evoked were inescapable and, although she said little, Tom was determined to share his excitement.

Perhaps he hoped that by talking about his afternoon he could persuade his mother that Ben was not the ogre she appeared to think him. He might even have imagined that she would become intrigued, and show some curiosity about the place herself.

But, in spite of a wilful stirring of her emotions, Jaime succeeded in remaining impassive, and it wasn't until Tom had gone to bed that the enormity of what was happening washed over her. Tom's words, his admiration, his innocent response to his first taste of what it was like to be rich, reminded Jaime so much of herself, of the way she had behaved over fifteen years ago. Like him, she had been overwhelmed by the trappings of wealth and influence, seduced by the idea of sharing that kind of life.

She had been eighteen when she met Philip Russell. He had come into the bar one night with a group of young people who were all staying at the old Priory. The Dunstans had owned it in those days. Sir Peter Dunstan had been a retired military man whose second, and much younger wife was constantly giving house parties for her London friends.

It had been Christmas Eve, Jaime remembered, and she had been home after completing her first term at university. She had intended to take a law degree, but of course that had all gone by the board when Philip came on the scene. She had liked him at first sight, and she had been absurdly flattered when he'd shown the feeling was mutual.

Her feelings had been understandable, she thought now, despite the shiver of revulsion that slid down her spine. He had been a good-looking man, with none of the loud-mouthed brashness of the other members of the group. He had seemed shy, retiring, with them, and yet not quite one of them. Jaime had actually sympathised with him, and Philip had responded to her encouragement.

And, during the months of their courtship, Jaime had had no reason to doubt her first impressions. On the contrary, he had always treated her with consideration and respect, and, unlike the boys she was used to going out with, Philip had never attempted to get her into bed.

Naturally, Jaime had appreciated the advantages his independent means had provided. As the elder son of an undoubtedly wealthy family, Philip had only played at working. He sat on various boards, and attended occasional meetings, but most of his time was spent in frivolous pursuits. He enjoyed skiing, and sailing, and shooting in the season. He enjoyed driving, and had several expensive cars garaged below his penthouse apartment in Belgravia. He was a typical gentleman—

or what Jaime presumed a gentleman should be—and, if her mother and father hadn't exactly approved of the relationship, they, too, had profited from the association.

Of course, his mother and father had openly disapproved. Philip had taken her once—and only once!—to meet his parents, at their home in London. It had been a disaster. Another young woman had been present, whom Jaime was left in no doubt had been expected to become Mrs Philip Russell, and what with her—Jaime's—nervousness, and Philip's embarrassment, the visit had been a nightmare.

Looking back, she realised that Heather—yes, that had been her name: Heather Sanders—had had a lucky escape. She could have had no idea of the kind of man Philip was, any more than Jaime. To all intents and purposes, he was a paragon, and that was why Jaime had considered herself so fortunate.

Oh, the enormous diamond ring he had bought her on their engagement, and the Porsche, which he had told her would be waiting for her when they returned from their honeymoon, had helped. She wouldn't have been human if she hadn't been excited at the prospect of marrying such a wealthy man. All her friends thought she had been immensely lucky, and she had basked in their envy right up to the wedding.

The knowledge that Ben Russell was Philip's brother had been an added bonus. She hadn't met him in the months leading up to the wedding, but she had seen him on television. At that time, Ben had been working for the BBC, and it had been something else to brag about—that her future brother-in-law was such a famous face.

How young she had been, thought Jaime bitterly. How naïve about life, and men. She had thought she knew it all, when in fact she had known nothing. Not about life, or emotions, or, most particularly, about the man she was planning to marry.

They had been married in the small church where Jaime had been christened, and where she had taken her first communion. In spite of the absence of most of the members of Philip's family, it had not been a small wedding. The fact that her father was the licensee of the Raven and Glass ensured that the church was full, and it was not until they were greeting guests at the reception that Jaime realised Philip's brother had attended. He hadn't been best man. One of Philip's friends from London—a man Jaime had never met before—had performed that duty, and when the tall dark man stepped in front of her she had had no premonition of the role he was to play in her life. On the contrary, her initial reaction had been one of apprehension. She had recognised him, of course. How could she not? But she had been wary of his intervention when Philip introduced them.

She hadn't needed to be. Ben hadn't come to scorn or cause trouble. Looking back now, she realised it had been kind of him to come at all. He hadn't had to. Certainly his parents had felt no such compunction. Apart from a few of Philip's friends, the majority of the guests were from Jaime's side of the family, but by putting in an appearance Ben had tacitly endorsed the occasion on behalf of the Russells.

For which she had been grateful, Jaime admitted wryly, remembering how proud she had felt when he'd stood and talked to her. Ben had a way of giving someone his whole attention when they spoke, and she couldn't deny she had been dazzled by his friendly personality.

His wife had not been with him. At age twenty-four, Ben had already been married for three years, but the elusive Mrs Russell preferred to remain in the background. Or so Philip said, when she asked him. Of course, that was before they left on their honeymoon, before other considerations swept such paltry cares aside.

It had taken Jaime just twenty-four hours to realise she had made a terrible mistake. Twenty-four hours, during which time she realised she did not know Philip at all. The shy, sensitive man she thought she had married didn't exist. The man who had taken her to bed in his apartment was a monster, and she couldn't believe the way he had treated her.

Oh, the following morning, the morning they were due to leave for their honeymoon in Bermuda, Philip had apologised profusely. When he saw the bruises on her face and neck—bruises that were repeated on her body, but were not all, thankfully, visible—he was contrite. It was the champagne, he said. He had drunk too much; he hadn't known what he was doing. She was so beautiful, he groaned, she had gone to his head.

Jaime hadn't been convinced. She was not that naïve. But she was his wife, they were married, and the idea of telling anyone else what had happened was not a viable proposition. After all, what if he was right? What if the champagne had gone to his head? How could she revoke her vows after only one night?

Luckily, the worst of the bruises were on her neck, and a scarf, twisted into the collar of her blue silk travelling suit, did not look out of place. For the rest, a rather heavier foundation than usual proved invaluable, and when they boarded the plane and took their seats in the first-class compartment Jaime succeeded in fooling herself that it was all going to be all right.

And Philip was his usual charming self. He spent the whole trip ensuring that she was comfortable, that she had everything she needed, and describing their destination so enthusiastically that Jaime couldn't help feeling a sense of anticipation. He had been so successful in soothing her fears that by the time they landed on the chain of islands, which were strung together with causeways to form the delightful colony of Bermuda, Jaime had convinced herself that what had happened the night before had been just an aberration.

They didn't stay at a hotel. Philip's parents owned a villa, and although they might not have approved of the marriage they had agreed to allow the young couple to use the colour-washed cottage that overlooked an unblemished stretch of coral sand.

It should have been heaven, but for Jaime it became a living hell. No matter how considerate Philip might be to her during the day, she could only think of the nights, and the fact that her worst fears had been realised. She had sometimes wondered if Philip's parents had known of his sexual perversions before the wedding. That would account for their apparent generosity in lending them the cottage. There was no way she and Philip could have stayed at a hotel without someone noticing Jaime's distress. Besides, how would he have explained her swollen face, or the dark discolourations on her body?

As it was, she had counted the days until they could go home. Home meant England, and the chance to escape from this mockery of a marriage. She didn't care now what her friends thought, or how humiliated she would feel to have to admit what had happened. She only wanted her freedom. To never have to see Philip again.

Strangely enough, she didn't tell Philip how she felt. Not then, at least. Something, some subconscious knowledge, perhaps, warned her not to confront him until she was back on her own ground. She didn't think he was mad. Most of the time he was too obscenely normal, treating her with such sickening sweetness that she wanted to vomit. But she was afraid of him, afraid of the power he had over her here, far from the protection of her family.

Then, the night before they were due to fly back to England, Philip told her what he would do if she ever told anyone what went on between them. He had friends, he said—friends she wouldn't like to know. He was not specific, but Jaime was left in no doubt as to what might happen if she attempted to leave him. He loved her, he said, and the ignominy of that remark was a small indication of how abnormal he was. He didn't love her. He didn't know the meaning of the word. But he wanted her, and he would do anything he had to do to keep her. And what she had hoped was just a term of detention became a life sentence.

Jaime closed her eyes now, as the horror of that evening in Bermuda surged over her again. She had lost control, of course. As he had probably guessed she would. He had chosen his time deliberately, and all the pain and humiliation of the last two weeks had burst out of her in a desperate flood of recrimination. She didn't remember what she'd said. But despair had made her reckless. This might be the last chance she had to say what she thought, and her anguish and agitation had sent her clawing for his face.

It wasn't until she saw the glittering sensuality in his eyes that she realised he was actually enjoying her assault. He was a big man—almost as tall as Ben, and more heavily built. He had fended her attack quite easily, and there had never been any danger of her doing him any permanent damage. On the contrary, she had seen, to her dismay, that he was quite violently aroused, and when he ripped her clothes from her, and flung her on the bed, he climaxed almost as soon as he thrust himself inside her.

Jaime didn't see her parents for two weeks after their return from that parody of a honeymoon. Philip made sure her face revealed no betraying bruises when he drove her down to Kingsmere for a visit. To all intents and purposes, they were an ideal couple. Both young, and tanned, and happy—as one would expect after spending two weeks in the sun.

If Jaime's eyes were a little hollow, and her clothes seemed a little loose on her tall frame, it was assumed that she and Philip had been burning the candle at both ends. Certainly, she did her best to ensure that her mother and father had no reason to suspect otherwise. She didn't trust Philip not to involve them should she become a problem, and she had come to the painful realisation that she had to live with her mistakes.

CHAPTER EIGHT

MARGARET HAINES phoned on Thursday evening. Tom was out, and when Jaime picked up the phone she had already steeled herself to speak to Ben. It was three days since that incident in the kitchen, and she was sure it wouldn't be another week before they heard from him again.

However, she was pleasantly surprised to hear Felix's ex-wife's voice—even if her thoughts immediately jumped to his present wife's condition. She should have phoned Maggie, and let her know, she thought unhappily. She deserved to know, and no one else was likely to tell her.

'Long time, no see,' Maggie remarked, after the initial greetings were over. 'How are you, Jaime? How's Tom?'

'Oh, we're OK.' Jaime responded quickly, wondering if Maggie had learned that Ben Russell was living in Kingsmere now. Like Felix, she knew that Jaime had been married to Philip Russell at one time, and, also like Felix, she had been told the tale that Tom was not Jaime's ex-husband's son. 'Tom's looking forward to the holidays, of course. Just another few weeks, and then he'll consider himself a fifth former.'

'A fifth former! Really?' Maggie made a sound of amazement. 'It doesn't seem any time since he was starting infant school.'

'I know.' Jaime laughed. 'But, believe me, it feels like it.'

'Why? Tom's not a problem, is he?' Maggie was concerned. 'He always seems such a nice boy. Unlike some of the tearaways I see walking along Gloucester Road.'

'Oh—well, he is. A nice boy, I mean.' Jaime had to choose her words with care. Although she was sure Maggie would be sympathetic, she was loath to discuss her present difficulties with anyone. It was foolish, she knew, but talking about it would only magnify the problem.

'So, it's just old age creeping on, is it?' Maggie teased her gently. 'It's a pity you've never let another man into your life. I've always thought you were an ideal mother.'

Jaime's lips twisted. 'Thank you.'

'No, I mean it.' Maggie sounded sincere. She paused, and then added cautiously, 'Don't you ever hear from Tom's father? I mean, he can't have been such a bad guy. Tom's far too nice for that.'

Jaime's fingers tightened round the receiver. She had to remember that, as far as Maggie was concerned, Tom's father was the reason she had broken up with Philip. Oh, what a tangled web I've woven, she thought ruefully. But before Ben's reappearance she had been managing more than adequately.

'No,' she lied now, crossing her fingers as she did so. 'No, I've no idea where he is. In any case, I'm quite happy as things are. As you say, I'm too old to start again.'

'That isn't what I said, and you know it,' Maggie retorted drily. 'These days women are having their first babies when they're older than you are. It's becoming quite the fashion—waiting until they're in their thirties to start a family.'

It was the ideal opening, and, deciding anything was better than talking about her own life, Jaime took it. 'I——' she began. It wasn't easy but it had to be said. 'I—did you know that—that Lacey——?'

'Is having a baby?' Maggie finished for her, and Jaime's breath escaped on a sigh. 'Yes, I know, my dear. As a matter of fact, Felix told me himself. The old fool thought I might be upset about it. As if I would! It's exactly what he needs to bring him to his senses.'

Jaime frowned. 'What do you mean?'

'Well, I know Felix of old, and he was never what I would describe as a natural father! My dear, when my two were little Felix spent all his time on the golf course. He couldn't stand changing nappies, or being woken up in the middle of the night. And from what I hear of Lacey I can't see her letting him get away scot-free.'

'Oh.' Jaime couldn't prevent a gurgle of amusement. 'And here was I worrying about how you'd take it.'

'Yes. Well, Felix obviously felt the same. But don't worry, Jaime. It is more than two years since the divorce, and believe it or not I'm beginning to appreciate my freedom.'

'I'm so glad.' Jaime meant it. 'So—tell me all your news.'

'Well, I will. But, actually, I wondered if you'd like to come to dinner tomorrow evening. It's ages since I've seen you, and I don't entertain very often. We could have a good old natter, and sink a bottle of booze. What do you say?'

Jaime had to laugh. 'I can't afford to sink any booze,' she protested hastily. 'Alcohol contains far too many calories, and I'm trying to cut down.'

'Rubbish.' Maggie was dismissive. 'You're not over-weight. You're just statuesque. Remember all those Rubens nudes? People knew about femininity in those days.'

'Well, it's nice of you to say so, but I really ought to lose a few pounds. But not tomorrow night,' Jaime agreed, accepting the invitation. 'What time do you want me? Half-past seven? Eight o'clock?'

'Half-past seven will do fine,' said Maggie comfortably. 'And why don't you take a cab? That way, you won't have to worry about having a few glasses of wine. I'd hate you to lose your licence and then blame me!'

Tom was rather ambivalent about his mother's proposed outing when she mentioned it at breakfast next morning. 'But what if anybody phones?' he exclaimed at once, and Jaime didn't need to be a mind-reader to guess who he was thinking of. 'I mean, I've promised to take Angie to the disco. There won't be anybody in if—if anyone should call.'

'Why don't you come right out and say it?' Jaime demanded, her own patience wearing a little thin at this point. 'You're afraid Ben Russell will phone, and there won't be anybody here to speak to him. Well, I'm sorry, but we can't live our lives waiting for—for your uncle to call!'

Tom hunched his shoulders. 'Well, he did say he'd ring later in the week,' he mumbled defensively. 'I thought he might invite me over there on Saturday.'

'To the Priory?' Jaime stared at him. 'Did he say he would?'

Tom's jaw jutted. 'Not in so many words.'

'So it's really your idea.'

'No.' Tom was indignant. 'He did say I could go there again.' He paused, and then added unwillingly, 'He said he was thinking of buying some horses. He asked me if I could ride.'

'And, of course, you said no.'

'Well, I can't, can I?'

Tom's expression was sulky, and Jaime wondered if Maggie would still think she was doing such a good job if she could see them now. She sighed. The trouble was, Tom's resentment wasn't entirely unjustified, and the knowledge that had he been brought up like his father, riding would have been just another of the options open to him, stung her conscience. Did she really have the right to obstruct their relationship? How would Tom feel, if he eventually learned the truth?

'All right,' she said, acknowledging that she was giving in to him more and more these days. She just hoped her capitulation wouldn't have a backlash. Tom knew he was winning, but he didn't know why.

'All right, what?' he asked now, and although Jaime realised her answer had been rather oblique Tom's face had brightened considerably.

'All right—you can go and see your uncle again, if he asks you,' she declared tersely. 'And don't worry about him ringing while you're out. He'll ring back. I have the feeling that—well, that he wants to see you again just as much as you want to see him.'

Jaime told herself it was worth the effort it had cost her to say that when she saw the delight on her son's face. Poor Tom, she thought. He so badly needed a man in his life. Oh, her father did his best, but he was so much older, and, besides, he had the pub to run. Which didn't leave a lot of time for his grandson, or the rest of the family either.

She was still thinking about this when she climbed into the taxi that evening. Although she was sure she could have driven herself home after the one or two glasses of wine she intended to drink at Maggie's house, she had decided not to take the risk. She needed her car to get to work, and to keep her and Tom mobile. If she lost her licence, she'd miss it terribly.

It began to rain as the taxi turned out of Dorset Road, and Jaime was glad she had chosen to wear a suit instead of a dress. Besides, the short skirt and extra-long jacket of the fine wool outfit were very flattering with her long legs, and she hadn't had many opportunities to wear it. Her own fault, of course, as Tom would say, and until Ben had come on the scene it hadn't been an issue.

Nevertheless, when she caught a glimpse of her reflection in the driver's rear-view mirror, she did feel quite pleased with her appearance. Black definitely suited her, she thought, fingering the neckline of the slim-fitting jacket. Particularly when it was teamed with a bronze silk camisole.

A faint smile tipped her lips before she caught the driver's eye and realised he had observed her self-appraisal. Immediately, she looked away, but his, 'Heavy date?' made some kind of response unavoidable.

'Not a date at all,' she admitted, wishing she weren't so prone to exhibiting her embarrassment. 'Just a meal with a friend.'

'Lucky friend,' commented the driver admiringly, his swarthy face creasing into a grin. 'And you can tell him I said so.'

Jaime opened her mouth to say it wasn't a 'him', and then closed it again. It wasn't important, after all. She wasn't likely to see the taxi driver again. And it made her feel good to think a stranger should find her attractive.

Maggie lived out towards Nettleford. It was the house she and Felix had occupied before the divorce, and was part of the settlement she had demanded. Jaime had often thought she wouldn't have wanted to go on living in a house which must hold so many unhappy memories, but Maggie seemed content. It was the house where her children had been brought up, she said, and she still loved it. Jaime suspected she still loved Felix, too, but that was something they never talked about.

The house stood on its own, just beyond the outskirts of the town. Jaime hadn't thought about it before, but it was only a couple of miles from the Priory, and she hoped Maggie wasn't going to spend the evening speculating about the new occupant. It would be ironic if, in hoping to avoid thinking about Ben, she found herself in the position of having to talk about him.

The rain was beating against the car windows as they turned between the gates of Maggie's house, and Jaime was glad she was going to be dropped off at the door. She wouldn't have fancied having to park the car and then run for cover. The heels she was wearing would not take kindly to the gravel of Maggie's forecourt, and as there were two cars parked in the driveway already it could have been a problem.

Jaime frowned as the significance of the two strange cars occurred to her. Maggie, she knew, drove a rather shabby Volvo, and unless she had changed her car in the last few weeks she had other guests.

Jaime tried not to feel disappointed. Maggie had said nothing about inviting anyone else when she had asked Jaime to dinner. But then, she hadn't actually said there was just to be the two of them, and it was Jaime's fault for jumping to conclusions. She was doing that a lot lately, she thought wryly. She might as well accept it: she was no clairvoyant.

All the same, she did look at the cars rather closely. But neither of them was of obviously German origin— like a Mercedes, for example. Deciding she was getting paranoid, Jaime identified a modest Rover, and a mid-range Ford, neither of which appeared to boast any high-tech characteristics. Probably the doctor and the vicar, she thought ruefully, leaning forward to pay her driver. She seemed to remember meeting Maggie's doctor on another occasion, and she resigned herself to an evening of small talk.

The door had opened while Jaime was settling her fare, and because it was such a dismal evening Maggie was silhouetted by the lights behind her. Unlike Lacey, Felix's first wife was a big woman, with generous breasts and thighs, and a total disregard for health food. She kept fit by exercising the two Dobermanns, which had taken the place of her grown children, and, in spite of her size, she was decidedly feminine.

'Hurry,' she called, as Jaime got out of the taxi. 'I was beginning to think you weren't coming.'

'Oh? Am I late?' Jaime exclaimed, after sprinting up the steps and into the house. She bent to give Maggie a damp kiss, and then pulled a wry face. 'Blame it on the weather!'

'Yes. Isn't it dreadful?' Maggie nodded, and closed the door. 'No wonder they say *flaming* June! Flaming awful, that's what I say.'

Jaime smiled. 'Well, it has been a pretty nice summer up until now,' she demurred, checking her hair in the mirror of a mahogany tallboy. And then, lowering her voice, 'You should have warned me you were having a dinner *party*. I thought there was just going to be the two of us.'

Maggie coloured. 'Well, you look pretty good to me,' she declared, avoiding Jaime's eyes by admiring her suit. 'That's new, isn't it? I don't believe I've seen it before——'

'Maggie!'

'Well, it's hardly a party,' protested the other woman quickly. 'There's just the four of us.'

'Four, hmm?' Jaime didn't know why, but already her nerves were prickling, and she chided herself for jumping to conclusions yet again. 'Who clsc is here?'

Maggie busied herself with brushing a pearl of rain-water from Jaime's sleeve, and ushered her across the hall to the drawing-room door. 'Come and see,' she said, without answering her, and although Jaime wanted to resist she had to go with her.

As she had anticipated, two men were waiting for them in the drawing-room, seated in the wing-chairs that faced one another across the wide hearth. Of course, there was no fire in the hearth this evening. The space was filled by an enormous bowl of dusky pink roses, whose fragrance overlaid the potent scents of good Scotch and fine tobacco. One of the men was smoking, Jaime noticed, as they both rose to their feet at her entrance, but it was hardly relevant. Her eyes were drawn to those of the other man, and the realisation that for once her instincts had not betrayed her was no compensation.

'You know John, don't you?' Maggie was saying fussily, and Jaime guessed she had some idea at least of how her friend was feeling. 'And—and Ben? You two have met, haven't you?'

'Frequently,' said Ben, as Jaime struggled to regain her composure. 'Hello, Jaime. You look nice.'

'Thank you.' Jaime got the words through her teeth with a supreme effort. She turned to his companion. 'Dr Fellowes.'

'Please—I thought we'd agreed you'd call me John,' exclaimed the elderly doctor, with a chuckle. 'Whenever I hear *Dr* Fellowes, it's usually followed by a request for a consultation!'

Jaime forced a smile. 'All right—John. I—isn't it an awful evening?'

'Terrible,' he agreed, pulling a face. 'Now, can I get you a drink, my dear?'

'Oh——' Jaime glanced uncertainly at Maggie '—well—yes. Just a small sherry, if you have one.'

'I'll leave John to look after you while I go and check on the food,' declared Maggie, with obvious relief, heading for the door. 'Sit down, Jaime. We don't stand on ceremony here.'

Jaime's gaze slid past Ben's lean face, and settled on the chintz-covered sofa. But as she seated herself, and crossed her slim legs, she was intensely conscious of his presence. She didn't have to look at him to be aware of him, or need a second glance to register every detail of his appearance. She already knew he was wearing dark blue trousers, and a matching corduroy jacket that accentuated the width of his shoulders. The sombre shade suited his dark colouring, too. He looked composed and relaxed, and undeniably attractive. But what troubled Jaime most was his disturbing familiarity.

But what was he doing here? Her eyes flickered in his direction and then, finding his eyes upon her, they flickered away again. Oh, God, she thought, why was he doing this to her? All right. So he wanted to see his son. She wasn't stopping him, was she? So why did he insist on haunting her like this?

To her relief, Ben reseated himself in the chair he had occupied before her arrival, but there was no way she could avoid answering him when he spoke to her. She didn't know what he had told Maggie and John Fellowes about their relationship, and she had no desire to arouse their curiosity.

His first question was innocent enough. 'Have you had a busy week?' he asked, his green eyes displaying what—to anyone else—could only be described as a mild interest, and Jaime was glad John chose that moment to hand her her sherry.

'I'm always busy,' she responded coolly, taking refuge in her glass. 'Mm——' she smiled up at the other man '—this is delicious!'

'What do you do exactly?'

Ben was tenacious, and, realising he was enjoying her discomfort, Jaime decided it was time to strike back. 'Don't you know?' she enquired politely, running the pad of her index finger around the rim of her glass. 'I thought you'd be familiar with the means of tax avoidance.'

John sucked in his breath, and even Ben's lips tightened, but his tone was just as tolerant as he persisted, 'Humour me.' And only Jaime was aware of the double-edged warning in his request.

'I'm sure—Jaime—doesn't want to talk about her work tonight,' John intervened, evidently deciding a mediator was required here. He lowered himself on to the sofa beside her, and patted the hand that was curled very tightly in her lap. 'Tell us about that handsome son of yours. Maggie says he'll be entering the fifth form next term.'

'That's right.' Jaime's tongue circled her upper lip. Of all the subjects to choose, she was thinking grimly, when Ben spoke again.

'How old is—your son?' His green eyes were openly challenging between the thick black lashes. 'You must have been expecting him when I left Kingsmere.'

'Must I?' Jaime refused to satisfy his rampant ego. 'When was that?'

Ben's features took on a dangerous expression. 'Oh, I'm sure you remember,' he said. 'My wife and I went to live in Africa about eighteen months after you and Phil got married.'

Jaime couldn't withstand his accusing stare, and she bent her head over the glass as John tried to restore some measure of concord to the debate. 'Of course,' he said, as if the thought had just occurred to him, 'you were married to Ben's brother, weren't you, Jaime? So—so Tom——' he looked to the other man for guidance '—Tom must be your nephew.'

A pregnant silence greeted this pronouncement, one which seemed to last a lifetime, but which probably lasted only a few seconds. Nevertheless, Jaime waited with bated breath for Ben's denial, knowing how casually he could remove the protection of the Russell name.

But it didn't come. Instead, Maggie's cheerful, 'Are we all ready to eat?' saved a potentially dangerous situation, and John turned to her eagerly, more than willing to abandon their discussion.

Not that Ben would have said anything to expose himself, Jaime told herself tensely. He was far too clever for that. But he could have removed the respectability of the Russell name from her, and she ought to feel grateful that he hadn't.

Ben's dark face was unreadable, however. As Jaime allowed Maggie to link arms and lead her into the dining-room, she could hear him exchanging small talk with John Fellowes behind them. It didn't seem to have bothered him that the conversation had taken such an embarrassing turn. Nor did he seem perturbed that he had left a significant question unanswered.

'You're all right, aren't you?' Maggie asked, in a low voice, revealing she was not unaware of the situation. 'Honestly, I didn't know John was bringing him! He asked if he could bring a friend, and naturally I said yes. How was I to know it would be your brother-in-law?'

'*Ex*-brother-in-law,' murmured Jaime tightly, and then forced a smile. 'It doesn't matter.'

'It does matter.' Maggie was not deceived by her attempt at indifference. 'I knew it would, dammit. Oh,

Jaime, I'm sorry. I wouldn't have upset you for the world!'

'Really, it's not that important.' Jaime squeezed the older woman's arm, as they separated to take their places at the table. 'Oh—this looks pretty,' she added, surveying the lace place-mats, and the centre-piece of roses and lilies. 'You're so clever with flowers. I'm no good at these arrangements.'

Maggie accepted her praise modestly, but it was obvious she was not convinced by Jaime's tactics. Nevertheless, there was nothing she could do but make the best of it, and Jaime knew it was mostly her own fault for allowing Ben to get under her skin. The fact that he had always been able to do so was no reassurance.

The food was excellent. Maggie was a good cook, and her salmon mousse was one of Jaime's favourites. This was followed by a delicous rack of lamb, and although she had been afraid she wouldn't be able to eat anything Jaime was able to acquit herself quite creditably.

It helped that the conversation at the table was fairly general. John Fellows possessed a fund of anecdotes about awkward patients he had treated, and even Ben joined in with some stories of his own. It was quite a novelty for Jaime to sit back and listen to Ben talking about the African veldt. He spoke about the wildlife, and the problems each country was having guarding against poachers. He described life in the game reserves, and the animal carnage he had seen in East Africa. And he also talked a little about the war in Ethiopia, and the terrible threat of famine that was never far away.

It was the first time since he'd come back that Jaime had been with him without feeling threatened by him— but she discovered the experience was no less disturbing. Until now, she had been so intent on keeping a barrier between them that she had never allowed herself to feel any normal emotions towards him. The fact that he had travelled widely, had had an interesting, and sometimes dangerous job, and was therefore a fascinating guest to have at any dinner table, had been obscured by her own distorted obsession with him. She had never permitted herself to consider that she could actually *like* him. She had been so intent on loving him and hating him that she hadn't seen the obvious alternative.

Or hadn't wanted to see, she reminded herself sharply. It was much easier to deal with strong emotions than cope with the insidious wiles of gentler ones. She didn't want to like Ben. She didn't want to see him as Maggie was seeing him, or admit that she was as interested in his work as anyone else at the table. He was Philip's brother, she told herself. He had seduced her, and betrayed her. He had left her expecting his child, and gone off to Africa with his wife. The fact that he hadn't known she was expecting his child was irrelevant. He had made it clear he had no intention of divorcing his wife for her, and Jaime had refused to use her condition to attempt to change his mind.

They had coffee in the drawing-room, by which time Jaime had convinced herself that any interest she had had in Ben's reminiscences had been spurious. She told herself it had been a combination of the food and the wine—particularly the wine—and the easy ambience of the conversation that had breached her guard and tumbled her defences. She didn't really care how Ben had spent the last fifteen years; nor did she want to think of the life he and Maura had led together. The insidious image of Ben stretched out on a bed with the other woman, making love to Maura, as he had once made love to her, could still strike a stabbing chord in her memory. She might not want to admit that this was so, but time—and bitter experience—couldn't always take away the pain.

'So—isn't this nice?'

Having served her guests with coffee, Maggie seated herself on the sofa beside Jaime. She was evidently delighted that the evening had not turned into the disaster she had half expected, and Jaime felt a twinge of sympathy for her. Now that it was almost over, she could imagine how her friend must have felt when Ben had arrived on her doorstep. Although Maggie didn't know the whole story, the fact that he was Philip's brother must have filled her with dismay. After all, *she* wouldn't have wanted to spend the evening with Felix's brother, particularly if her association with his family had been as acrimonious as Jaime's with Philip's.

'You must give me the recipe for that orange sorbet,' Jaime murmured now, eager to keep the conversation to impersonal matters. 'I don't think I've ever tasted anything more delicious. Where did you find it?'

'Oh—I got it out of some magazine or other,' exclaimed Maggie modestly. 'I wouldn't like to say which one. I buy so many.'

'Maggie's a magazine-addict,' put in John Fellowes drily. 'The local church does famously out of her contributions to its jumble sales.'

'Well, I have to do something,' she protested. 'I don't read—well, not books, anyway—and I don't like gardening. I'm not like Jaime. I don't—have...'

And then, shaking her head, she faltered to a stop. Her cheeks were pink with confusion, and it was obvious what she was thinking. She had realised that what she had been about to say could embarrass her guest, and rather than go on with it she got up and offered more coffee.

But it was too soon, and they all knew it, and as if to rescue the situation Ben said quietly, 'I'm sure we all have vices we're not too proud of. I know I do.' He looked at Jaime. 'Don't you agree?'

But Jamie had had just about as much as she could take for one evening. 'I think I ought to be going,' she said, instead of answering him, dragging her gaze away from his, and addressing Maggie. 'Um—Tom will be home soon, and I don't like him going into an empty house.'

'Of course.' Maggie didn't argue, probably as relieved to break up the party as Jaime was. 'I'll go and call you a cab. I wonder if it's still raining.'

'There's no need to call Jaime a cab,' Ben inserted swiftly, getting to his feet. 'I'll take her home.'

'Oh, no—really...'

Jaime's anxious gaze flashed from Maggie to Ben, and back again. If only she had insisted on bringing her own car, she thought desperately. As it was, unless Maggie could come up with some significant excuse why Ben shouldn't take her home, she had no valid reason for refusing. It wasn't as if she felt the slightest bit woozy. The tension of the last few minutes had sobered her more completely than several cups of Maggie's strong black coffee could have done.

'Do you think it's wise to risk driving across town and back again when you've been drinking, Ben?' Maggie ventured now, revealing she had interpreted Jaime's message loud and clear. 'I mean, that's why Jaime didn't bring her own car. They're very strict about these things nowadays. Not like before you went to Africa...'

'I don't think what Ben's drunk this evening would put him over the limit,' the old doctor remarked con-sideringly, and Jaime wished, rather unfairly, that he would keep his nose out of her affairs. 'Besides, you'll wait hours for a taxi on a night like this. You know how busy they'll be.'

'Thank you, John.'

Maggie's sarcasm was lost on him, however, and although she accompanied her words with a killing look it was too late. The damage was done. Jaime had to choose between letting Ben take her home—which surely couldn't be as harrowing as she was anticipating—and staying here, at the mercy of his edged comments, for a possibly indefinable period.

'Well,' she said, clearing her throat, and the ad-mission almost choked her, 'if—if Ben—doesn't mind...'

'My pleasure,' said Ben smoothly, sliding his hand into his jacket pocket, and pulling out his car keys. 'It's been a very pleasant evening, Maggie. I hope you'll forgive me if I curtail it a little.'

'Of course.' Maggie looked unhappily at Jaime. 'If—er—if it weren't for Tom, you could have stayed the night.'

'But there is Tom, isn't there?' Ben put in, before Jaime could say anything. 'And Jaime takes her ma-ternal duties very seriously, don't you?' His eyes chal-lenged her to deny it. 'So—shall we go?'

CHAPTER NINE

BEN'S car was the Ford Sierra, and he insisted on fetching it to the door so that Jaime could just run down the steps and get inside. It was still raining, and drops of moisture sparkled on Ben's hair as he leaned across the passenger seat to open the door for her.

'I'll ring you next week,' Maggie called, as Jaime got into the car, and she stood at the door, waving, as Ben swung the vehicle round in a half-circle and down the waterlogged drive.

It really was a filthy night. The rain was coming down in sheets, and the wipers had to work overtime to keep the windscreen clean. But it also narrowed Jaime's world to the heated confines of the car, and she couldn't help but be aware of Ben's lean frame only inches from her own.

Not that Ben was showing any interest in her. His attention was focused on the road ahead, and she was annoyed with herself for allowing his presence to disconcert her in any way. He was giving her a lift home, that was all. And judging by the slickness of the road she ought to be grateful she was not having to put her safety in the hands of some untried driver.

Nevertheless, she was aware of him. Her eyes were drawn to the hands handling the wheel so expertly, and the narrow wrists that emerged from the sleeves of his jacket. Was his skin warm? she wondered, her tongue lingering at the corner of her mouth. How was he adapting to this much cooler temperature, after so many years spent in a tropical climate? That was one thing he hadn't spoken about; that, and his wife.

She tore her eyes away, and tried to concentrate on the night outside. They were crossing the town now, and, as Dr Fellowes had said, there were plenty of people waiting for taxis. It probably would have been next to impossible to get one of them to come out to Maggie's house during the next hour or so, and her reluctance to accept this ride seemed extremely churlish in retrospect.

'I—didn't know you knew Dr Fellowes,' she murmured, feeling obliged to make some recompense, but loath to thank him outright, and Ben shrugged.

'You don't know much about me at all,' he responded, and his tone was as cool as hers now. 'Is it important?'

Jaime sighed. 'Not—not intrinsically, no.' She paused, and the disturbing memory of what her mother—and Tom—had said reared its ugly head again. 'Are—are you a patient of his?'

Ben slowed at a junction, and scanned the road ahead. 'I think that comes under the heading of a personal question,' he replied shortly. 'Are you?'

'Am I what?'

'A patient of Fellowes'.'

Jaime was confused. 'What has that got to do with anything?'

'Exactly.' Ben accelerated along Gloucester Road. 'Whether or not I'm a patient of John Fellowes has nothing to do with you.'

Jaime held up her head. 'I—I—was——'

'Curious?'

'No.' Jaime was indignant. 'I was—concerned.'

'Oh, come on.' Ben cast her a sardonic sideways glance. 'I think I've got the picture of what you think of me, and "concerned" doesn't come into it.'

'That's not true.' Jaime spoke rashly, and then struggled to justify her words. 'I mean—naturally, I'm concerned if—if you're ill——'

'Because you have Tom to consider, right?' Ben sounded bitter. 'You don't want him associating with me if I'm incubating some awful unsociable disease——'

'I never thought of that!' Jaime gazed at him defensively. 'I—I wouldn't dream of stopping him associating with you, because I might think you—you——'

'Had Aids?' he supplied grimly, and Jaime felt as if someone had sucked all the air from her body.

'If—if that's what's wrong with you,' she got out unsteadily, 'I—I know you wouldn't do anything to harm your own son.'

Ben's lips twitched. 'Isn't it rich!' he grated savagely. 'I have to threaten to be dying before you'll admit that Tom's my son!'

Jaime's throat constricted. 'You're—you're not dying,' she protested, realising how devastated she would feel if he were. 'There—there are experiments going on, treatments you can have...'

'If I had Aids,' agreed Ben flatly, bringing the Sierra to a halt, and Jaime saw with some astonishment that they had stopped outside her house. She hadn't been aware of anything for the last few minutes.

'*If* you had Aids?' she ventured blankly, and Ben gazed at her with a scornful expression.

'Yes,' he said evenly. 'I'm sorry to disappoint you, but I managed to avoid contracting any real life-threatening infections while I was in Africa. You'll have to save your dubious sympathies for some other poor sod, hmm?'

'You—*pig*!'

All the pent-up emotions of the evening exploded in a sudden surge of violence, and Jaime's hand connected heavily with his cheek. She knew it must have hurt him. Her own fingers stung quite painfully, and she was half prepared to admit she hadn't intended to hit him quite so hard. But, before she had a chance to make any kind of apology, Ben's hand circled the back of her neck, and he yanked her towards him.

'If that's the way you want to play it,' he muttered, before his mouth met hers, and although she tried to resist him he was much, much stronger than she was.

Besides, the line between anger and desire was a fine one. Anger was passion, and the whole evening had been one of suppressed emotion, of one sort or another. When Ben took hold of her, when his hard fingers dug into her nape, and his angry mouth found hers, instinct took over. She wanted to sustain her feelings, she wanted to despise him for allowing her to even think he might be dying; but those same emotions got in the way.

His mouth on hers was so insistent, savage at first, and then achingly persuasive. His tongue against her lips was hot and wet and persistent, and, although she held out for a few moments, he eventually coaxed her lips to part.

'We—we can't,' she gasped, when his tongue plunged into her mouth and she felt his hand gripping her thigh below the short skirt of her suit. 'Ben, someone might see us!'

His lips dragged across her cheek. 'You mean Tom, don't you?' he exclaimed harshly against her ear. His teeth dug painfully into her earlobe. 'Why don't you admit it?'

'I—all right,' she stammered, covering the hand that was sliding insistently along her thigh with both of hers. 'I mean Tom. I—won't do this to him.'

'Do what?' Ben lifted his head to look down at her, and in the muted light from the streetlamps his expression was vaguely menacing. 'Tell him the truth for once?' he taunted scathingly. 'Admit that you were once human enough to need a normal sexual relationship with a man?'

'With a married man,' Jaime reminded him tensely, and Ben made a sound of impatience.

'A man who cared about you just as much as you cared about him,' he retorted roughly. He looked down at her paltry attempt to stay his hand, and deliberately proved how useless that was. 'Don't try to stop me, Jaime,' he muttered, moving his hand beneath the hem of her skirt. 'You wouldn't succeed, and we both know why.'

'No.' Jaime twisted her head from side to side. 'Ben— please!'

'I will,' he promised unsteadily, and any further protest she might have uttered was stifled by the hungry pressure of his mouth.

Jaime's head swam. She tried to tell herself it was the celibate life she had been leading that was making her so vulnerable to his demands, but it wasn't that simple. The truth was, Ben was the only man who had ever made her feel this way, and when he cupped her face between his hands, and pressed her back into the seat, she clutched his neck with trembling fingers.

Ben's kiss lengthened and deepened. His tongue possessed her, filling her mouth with its hot, wet invasion. She felt weak, and breathless, dizzy with the need to keep some hold over a situation that was rapidly moving out of control. His jacket was open, and the warm male smell of his body filled her senses. His heart was hammering, matching hers for speed, and when her arms slid round his neck, and her breasts pushed against his chest, he uttered an anguished groan.

'Oh, God!'

The shuddering breath Ben gave, as he hauled himself back from her, was an indication of the effort it had taken. Slumping in his seat, he raked back his hair with hands that were shaking rather badly, pulling at his collar that suddenly seemed too tight.

Jaime's reactions were slower. Ben's withdrawal had been so sudden that she half expected to find Tom peering at them through the misted windows. But they were still alone. The rain had kept most people indoors, and the condensation on the car windows still gave them a flimsy kind of privacy. Which meant it had been his decision to put an end to the embrace, and humiliation washed over her, hot and shameful.

As she struggled up in her seat, Ben's sardonic, 'I rest my case,' was the final straw. But, when she would have thrust open her door and scrambled out, his hand caught her wrist. 'I'm sorry,' he muttered, and, although it would have been easier to tell him to go to hell, Jaime was tired of running away from her problems.

'Just—stay away from me in future,' she said, gritting her teeth. 'Don't imagine—*this*—gives you any leverage where I'm concerned. All right. Tom's your son. I've admitted it. But that affair was over long ago. And it's not just the drink-driving laws that have changed since you went away. Women have changed; *I've* changed. We're not ashamed of our sexuality any more. We can meet men on equal terms. And just because I might fancy going to bed with you doesn't mean I feel some—some lifelong commitment!'

'That's what you think, is it?'

In the streetlights, Ben's face was hard, and she felt a quiver of apprehension. As she had spoken, the weary lines of remorse he had shown earlier had given way to a harsh cynicism, and she was uncomfortably aware of the weakness of her argument.

But she had to be resolute. 'Yes. It's what I think,' she lied bravely, wincing as his thumbnail scored her wrist. 'I—I won't stop Tom from seeing you, but leave me out of it.'

'And—Phil?'

'Phil?' Jaime swallowed. 'What about Philip?'

'Indeed.' Ben's lips twisted. 'What about Philip?'

Jaime's lips compressed for a moment. 'You're threatening to tell him, is that it?' she demanded, feeling the hot tears of desperation behind her lids. Was he to leave her no measure of self-respect at all? 'Well—I can't stop you, can I?' She dashed her hand across her eyes. 'If that's what turns you on, I suppose——'

'Phil's dead!' Ben's bitter announcement cut into her words, and with a gesture of contempt he thrust her wrist back into her lap. 'That's what I came to tell you, that night you were out and Tom let me in.' He made a sound of derision. 'You might say—subsequent events—got in the way.'

Jaime didn't remember getting out of the car and walking into the house. She did remember hearing the sound of the Sierra's engine as it roared away into the night, but that was after she had closed the door and was leaning numbly against it.

Philip was dead! she told herself weakly. The man who had had such a destructive influence on her life was gone! He couldn't hurt her any more.

Pushing herself away from the door, she walked rather shakily along the hall and into the kitchen. She needed a drink, she thought, putting her bag down on the table and riffling through the cupboards for the bottle of brandy she usually only used at Christmas. She needed something to fill the empty space inside her, and a strong glass of cognac seemed the appropriate choice.

But even after she had swallowed a mouthful of the fiery liquid, she still felt hollow, and, sitting down at the kitchen table, she tried to remember exactly what Ben had said. The trouble was, it had been pitiably little, and only now did she realise that she hadn't even asked for any of the details. She didn't know how he had died, or when. She didn't even know where he had been living. But Ben knew. Ben had known all along. And he had chosen to keep that information from her.

She gulped another mouthful of the brandy, coughing as it burned her throat. So far the spirit had had no beneficial effects on her whatsoever, and she wondered why people spoke so highly of its remedial qualities. All it was doing for her was making her feel sick.

But not sick enough to ignore the fact that Ben had deliberately kept the news of Philip's death from her. More than that, he had used her acknowledged fear of his brother for his own ends. He had known she would do anything to keep Tom's identity a secret, and because of that he had been able to insinuate himself into their lives.

God, he was despicable, she thought bitterly. He knew, better than anyone, what Philip's death would mean to her, and he had continued to hold the spectre of that painful relationship over her. Were all the Russells tarred with the same brush? Did they all enjoy exacting punishment of one sort of another?

But no. She refused to believe that. After all, Tom was a Russell, and he wasn't a monster. Until Ben had come on the scene, he had never gone against her wishes, and even now his conscience was giving him a hard time.

And Ben...

With a weary sigh, she propped her head in her hands. She didn't really believe Ben was like Philip. Oh, she would never forgive him for keeping Philip's death from her, but she couldn't forget that without Ben's help she might have suffered even more.

Looking back, she realised that Ben was the only person who could have helped. Philip's parents—*their* parents—were indifferent to the kind of life Jaime was leading. They had not wanted her to marry their son, and as far as they were concerned she didn't exist. Philip still saw his parents, but she never did. That was why she was so astonished when Ben came to the apartment.

It was Christmas Eve, and she and Philip had been married for almost six months. Because they were living in London, Jaime seldom saw her own family either. Which was just as well, in the circumstances. She knew her father could never have ignored his daughter's misery.

She had been pathetically grateful to see Ben, she remembered. It was so long since she had seen a really friendly face. Philip was out. He had often been out, though she didn't often go with him. Not that Jaime minded that. She was so ashamed of how she looked most of the time that going out at all had become a trial.

So, when Ben rang from the lobby downstairs and asked if he could come up, Jaime was delighted. Dismissing Philip's dour-faced housekeeper, she had answered the door herself, and it wasn't until she had let him in, and had seen him looking at her so strangely, that she realised she had forgotten to put on her make-up.

She almost always wore make-up these days. It was the only way she could bear to look at her face. She had become adept at hiding bruises beneath a dusky eye-shadow or a bronze blusher, and although her eyes were hollow they just gave her a haunted look. Or so she had believed.

But looking at Ben, she had seen the stunned realisation in his eyes. And even then her first reaction had been to dismiss it. She had fallen, she said, getting out of the shower. She was such a clumsy creature; Philip was losing patience with her.

It hadn't worked, and although at the time she had been terrified of what Philip might do Ben had refused to take no for an answer. After coaxing at least part of the truth from her, he had insisted she go and pack some clothes, and before driving her to her parents' home in Kingsmere he had taken her to see a friend of his in Harley Street. She remembered that she had still been protesting when he'd ushered her into the elegant waiting-room, though her will to resist any kind of pressure had been crucified in the months she had lived as Philip's wife.

His friend, a woman doctor, had made her take off all her clothes, and Jaime had stood in an agony of embarrassment as every mark on her body was questioned and noted. There had been no point in lying. She had too many bruises, many of them in places where the marks of other bruises were still visible. But it was humiliating nevertheless, and she was horrified when the woman produced an instamatic camera, and told her she was going to make a permanent record of what she had seen.

'If I don't, and the bruises fade, what proof will you have?' she asked practically. 'Believe me, whether we use them or not, they are necessary.'

And, because Ben had endorsed what the doctor had said, Jaime had gone through with it. She had put all her faith in him at the time, and it had not been misplaced. She never knew what he said to Philip, or whether her ex-husband was ever shown the photographs the doctor had taken. All she knew was that the threat Philip had represented had been removed, and she was eternally grateful to Ben for his support.

In the months that followed she saw Ben several times. Oh, she had probably enjoyed those occasions more than he did, she reminded herself painfully, but then, she hadn't been thinking too sensibly in those days. In her eyes he could do no wrong, and even her mother's warnings—about his relationship to Philip, and the fact that he was a married man—had fallen on deaf ears.

Looking back, she had to admit that Ben's reasons for visiting her had usually had a legitimate purpose. He had acted as Philip's intermediary, and it was through him that she had learned that Philip had agreed to stay away from her. She wanted a divorce, but that would have to wait until the required amount of time had passed, and for the present she was content to trust in Ben's protection.

His *protection*!

Jaime shivered. If only she had known then what she knew now, she thought ruefully. She had exchanged one kind of bondage for another. But that wasn't fair. Tom had never been a burden. And although she hated Ben, he had not been entirely to blame.

She remembered it had been almost exactly a year after she and Philip had parted when her friendship with Ben had been destroyed, forever. It was odd, she thought, how Christmas had played such an unhappy role in her life. It was at Christmas that she had met Philip, and Christmas when they had parted. So it was probably only fitting that that particular time of year should have provided such a disastrous end to her association with his brother.

But, at the time, she had had no inkling of the part he was to play in determining her future. In the year since he had 'rescued' her from Philip she had come to know him quite well—or so she had thought—and the anxiety she had first felt, when he appeared on her doorstep, had long since given way to a happy anticipation. Although she had other friends, he was the only person with whom she could be completely herself, and because he knew everything about her relationship with Philip she didn't have to pretend with him.

In retrospect, she supposed she had been foolish. After one devastating experience she should have been aware of the dangers she was courting. Ben was married, and although he seldom spoke of his wife he had never given any inclination that he was unhappy with his lot.

None the less, Jaime had begun to look forward to his visits with increasing excitement. He usually arrived at lunchtime, and because the pub was such a busy place he invariably took her out for a meal. It gave them an opportunity to speak privately, and if what he had to say only took up a small part of the time it never seemed to matter.

He told her about his work, and the people he worked with, and Jaime confided her own hopes and aspirations in the secretarial course she was taking. But Ben had always had a gift for narration, and Jaime always sat, entranced, while he described the places he had visited, and the events he had reported upon.

She never thought their relationship was moving beyond that of casual acquaintances. It didn't occur to her how strange it was that she and Ben should find such pleasure in each other's company. That the pretexts he used to promote each meeting were becoming ever more flimsy simply didn't register. Nor did the increasing frequency of those visits arouse any fears.

Then, just a few days before Christmas, Ben arrived in the afternoon. He said he had no especial reason for visiting her—except that he had brought her a small present—but he had been in the neighbourhood, and he wondered if she would join him for dinner.

Innocent enough, Jaime thought now, remembering her feelings then. She must have been crazy, she mused. It had never even occurred to her to refuse.

Of course, her parents hadn't been keen. Even though Ben had proved himself such a good friend over the past year, they were still suspicious of anyone called Russell. But Jaime refused to listen to their advice. Ben had asked her out to dinner, and all she could think of was what she was going to wear.

She supposed she must have been half in love with Ben even then. There seemed no other explanation for the way she had behaved. Or perhaps she had just been desperate for affection, she reflected bitterly. Certainly she had made it easy for him.

She didn't think of it before Ben came to collect her, but when he told her he was staying at the Crown Hotel she realised that, for once, he wasn't driving home after visiting her. She remembered wondering if his wife knew where he was this evening, and then dismissing the thought as being unworthy of consideration. In all honesty, she hadn't cared what his wife thought, which probably made what happened after a fitting punishment. But, at the time, she had been blind to anything but the delight of being with Ben.

Because it was Christmas week everywhere was busy, and after a noisy meal in town Ben suggested they go back to his hotel for a nightcap. In her more charitable moments, Jaime had to admit that the idea of having it in his suite had been as much her idea as his. But the bar at the Crown had been hectic, and the knowledge that Ben had a perfectly good sitting-room upstairs seemed too attractive to ignore.

Jaime had never been upstairs in the Crown before, and she was impressed with Ben's suite, which had a sitting-room, dressing-room, bedroom, and bathroom.

While they waited for a waiter to bring their drinks, she asked if she could use the bathroom, and Ben gave her a teasing grin before saying, 'Be my guest.'

When she came out again, she could hear Ben talking to the waiter in the sitting-room, and, on impulse, she went through the doorway that led into his bedroom. She told herself she was curious to see how the room was decorated, but it wasn't really that. It was the first time she had been in a man's bedroom since her break-up with Philip, and she was anxious to know how she would react to it. The fact that it was also the room where Ben was going to sleep tonight intrigued her, and when she saw a maroon silk dressing-gown lying on the end of the huge four-poster bed she couldn't resist running her fingers over the fine fabric.

'Did you find what you were looking for?'

Ben's voice from behind her brought her round with a start. She hadn't heard the waiter leave, but evidently he had, because Ben was now standing in the bedroom doorway.

Jaime's face suffused with colour. 'I—yes,' she said, her nail catching on the cloth as she withdrew her hand. 'Um—I'm sorry. I was just—looking around.'

'That's all right.'

Ben propped his shoulder against the door-frame. He was looking at her with his intense green eyes, and Jaime felt a *frisson* of fear slide along her spine. She should never have looked in here, she thought, never stepped inside. Now Ben was between her and freedom, and it wasn't easy not to panic.

Her palms were damp, and she tried to dry them out on the seat of the slim velvet trousers she was wearing. She had thought the soft trousers, worn with a full-sleeved satin blouse, both in a subtle shade of violet, were an attractive combination. But now she felt as exposed as if they'd suddenly become transparent.

'Do you realise this is the first time we've been alone together?' Ben remarked, when she said nothing, and she wondered how he could be unaware of her feelings. 'Apart from the car, of course,' he went on. 'But that's not quite the same.'

Jaime swallowed. 'So?'

The word came out high, and squeaky, and Ben's eyes darkened. 'So—nothing,' he said flatly. 'What's wrong?'

Jaime shook her head. 'What could be wrong?' she parried. 'Did—er—did the waiter bring our drinks?'

Ben stared at her. 'Yes. He brought them,' he answered. And then, roughly, 'For God's sake! Why are you looking at me like that? What do you think I'm planning to do? Rape you?'

Jaime held up her head. 'It has been done,' she got out unsteadily, and Ben uttered an angry oath.

'Not by me!' he exclaimed, and then, just when she thought he was going to leave her in disgust, he pushed himself away from the door and came towards her. 'I'm not Philip,' he said harshly, halting right in front of her. He cupped her quivering chin with one hand, and turned her face up to his. 'I'd never hurt you, Jaime. Surely you know that. For God's sake, I care about you too much for that.'

'Oh, Ben...'

Jaime could hardly bear to look at him. She felt sick and ashamed for doubting him. He wasn't Philip. He was nothing like Philip. And, although she had no real proof, she instinctively knew she could trust him.

Acting purely on impulse, she turned her head, and pressed her lips against his palm. His skin tasted warm, and salty, and essentially male, and, although she tried to prevent it, an errant tear trembled on her lashes.

'Hey...' Ben's voice was a little uneven now, and although he drew his hand away his thumb brushed abrasively across her lips. 'Don't cry!' he protested. 'Do you want people to think I'm a louse?'

Jaime lifted her hand to touch his face. 'They wouldn't think that,' she assured him huskily. 'I'm sorry. I guess I'm not much of a woman, am I?'

Ben captured her hand in his, and she knew his instincts were to thrust it back at her. But her words caused a spasm of frustration to cross his lean features, and almost against his will he pressed her open hand against his cheek.

'Don't say that,' he told her gruffly. 'Don't let one bad experience ruin your life. You're a warm, loving, beautiful woman. And I wouldn't be human if I wasn't aware of it!'

Jaime's tongue trembled against her upper lip. 'And are you?' she whispered. 'Aware of it—of *me*, I mean? You're not just saying it.'

Ben groaned. 'No, I'm not just saying it,' he declared, on an uneven breath. 'For God's sake, Jaime, don't do this to me—to us! We're friends. Don't—spoil it.'

Jaime's eyes showed her hurt. Drawing her hand away, she balled her fist, and pressed it into her palm. Of course, she thought unsteadily, Ben was married. He wasn't really interested in her. He was just being kind. And she wasn't making it easy for him.

'I—I should be going,' she said, looking anywhere but into his dark, defeated face. 'Heavens——' she glanced at her watch—the plain gold watch her parents had given her on her eighteenth birthday, and not the jewelled Rolex Philip had insisted on her wearing, and which she had left behind in London '—it's half-past ten! I wonder if the doorman can get me a taxi?'

'*Jaime!*'

The way Ben said her name should have warned her. But it didn't. She was so intent on extricating herself from what had become an humiliating situation that the idea that Ben might actually mean what he said didn't occur to her. She thought he was just being nice. She thought he was trying to save her embarrassment. But, in fact, she couldn't have been more wrong.

'Jaime,' he said again, as she would have gone past him, stepping into her path with sober intent. 'Jaime, don't go.'

'What?' Her nervous gaze flickered over his face and away again. 'Don't be silly. I've got to. It's late and—and I——'

But, as she spoke, his hand had taken hold of her arm, sliding from the narrow bones of her forearm to the quivering muscles of her biceps. And he had bent his head to press his lips against her shoulder, his tongue moistening the flesh through the folds of satin.

'Ben...'

Her use of his name was less certain, and as he continued to hold her against him all her limbs grew shaky.

What did he want of her? she wondered raggedly, and memories of the way Philip had used her returned to flood her mind with terror. Philip had been gentle once, she remembered. In those early days it had pleased him to pretend that this time he wouldn't hurt her, but she had very soon learned that his words were just more lies. Later on, he hadn't even pretended. He had known he was just wasting his time, and she shuddered at the thought of what he had done to her.

And, as if her trembling limbs had communicated her fear to Ben, he lifted his head. 'I'm not hurting you, am I?' he asked, and the anguish in his face made her swiftly shake her head.

'No.'

'But you're still afraid of me, aren't you?'

Jaime caught her breath. 'Not—not really——'

'Oh, Jaime!' His hand slid over her shoulder to mould the nape of her neck. 'Jaime, you have no idea how much I want you!'

And then his mouth was on hers, and all her anxious fancies disappeared beneath the searching pressure of his lips. With infinite tenderness he brought his other hand to her waist, drawing her fully against him. Then, with his thumb brushing the underside of her breast, he coaxed her lips to part.

Jaime's head was swimming, and his touch made all her limbs tingle. It wasn't like when Philip kissed her, even though, in the beginning, he had pretended to be gentle. With Philip, she had always been aware of his impatience and, afterwards, she had been amazed he had been able to fool her for so long. No wonder he had never attempted to get her to go to bed with him before they were married. She had thought he had too much respect for her. How dreadfully wrong she had been.

Ben's passion was different. She didn't know how she knew, but she did. The kisses he bestowed upon her lips were warmly possessive, but she welcomed them; his tongue, sliding between her teeth, was like hot velvet in her mouth. There was no pain, no subjugation; he wasn't trying to punish her—he was simply showing her how it should be.

And his tenderness destroyed any lingering doubts she might have had. Instead of pushing him away, she found herself winding her arms around his neck, and pressing herself eagerly against him. She was a normal human being after all, she thought, revelling in the realisation that Philip had not destroyed her ability to respond to her emotions. For so long she had believed she would never be able to let a man touch her without feeling the intense revulsion Philip had inspired. But suddenly she was free, and the feeling was intoxicating.

Of course, looking back, she supposed she had been at least half to blame for what happened. She had known Ben was married just as well as he did, and if she had had some crazy notion that he might leave his wife for her he had never said as much.

But maybe they had both been too caught up in the events of the moment to consider the rights and wrongs of what was happening. Ben had made his protest earlier on, but she hadn't listened to him. And if she still maintained that he was the stronger, that he should have been in control, perhaps she was being a little naïve. How could she have known how it would be between them? Who could have foretold the fire they would ignite?

They stood there, swaying in the doorway, while Ben covered her face with kisses. He kissed the high arch of her cheekbones, and the gentle curve of her chin. He teased her nose, and explored the silky contours of her ear, and closed her eyes with the feather-light brush of his tongue. But Jaime liked it best when his mouth returned to hers. Their lips fused together, and the plunging motion of his tongue aroused a trembling need inside her.

Her limbs were weak, and between her legs she could feel a dampness that was as disturbing as it was unfamiliar. She was filled with an aching longing to be even closer to him, and for the first time she realised the power of her own body.

'God, Jaime...'

Ben's voice was hoarse, and she remembered feeling enchanted that she could do this to him. She had never felt this way before, and when he moved her back against the door, and pressed his body against hers, she had no fear of the heavy thrust of his erection.

Even when he took her hand, and pushed it down between them, she felt no sense of panic. Ben's body didn't frighten her. She wasn't afraid of anything he might do to her. On the contrary, she wanted to please him, and her touch was firm and caressing.

And Ben was not proof against such blatant encouragement. His own hands slid up beneath the hem of her blouse, finding the fullness of her breasts confined by her cotton bra. He took the firm mounds into his hands, bending his head to caress their hard peaks through the layers of clothes that covered them. His tongue wet the material, so that when Jaime looked down she could see her nipple clearly outlined beneath. It caused a queer sensation in the pit of her stomach that was at once a pleasure and a pain. But it wasn't like any pain she had experienced before, and she realised she was shaking.

'You're beautiful!' Ben's husky words sounded more erotic than anything she had ever heard before. Holding her eyes with his, his fingers disposed of the buttons of her blouse, and exposed the bra beneath. 'I want to look at you,' he said. 'I want to look at all of you.' He released the strap of the bra. 'Will you let me?'

Jaime couldn't have refused, even if she'd wanted to. Her mind had ceased to function, beyond obeying the wild dictates of her body. She felt dazed, light-headed, totally absorbed with what Ben was doing to her. The world, and everything outside this room, had ceased to exist. Time wasn't important. All that she wanted was here, before her. All she needed was within her grasp.

Her blouse fell to the floor, followed swiftly by her bra, but she was hardly aware of it. Ben was touching her breasts, sucking her nipples, grinding his hips against hers. She knew what he wanted, because it was what she wanted, too. The miracle had happened: she was alive, she was responsive, and she was in love.

She hardly remembered how they got to the bed. She did recall the coolness of the coverlet against her back, and the feeling of wantonness she had experienced when Ben peeled the velvet trousers from her legs. She also remembered how he had pressed his face against the damp triangle of curls that protected her womanhood, and how she had opened her legs in shuddering abandon...

Jaime shivered as the memories swept over her. She might hate Ben for leaving her alone when she needed him most, but she couldn't deny that he had made her feel like a woman again. Those months with Philip had taken their toll in more ways than one. Because Philip had shown so little respect for her—and she had let him—she had also lost respect for herself. She had begun to believe his estimate of her, and she had never known what it was like to share the pleasures of making love. Ben had given her that, if nothing else.

Not that such thoughts had occupied her, as Ben tore off his own clothes. His jacket and tie were flung carelessly on to the floor, and several buttons from his shirt went skittering across the room. He undressed quickly, economically, as if he was afraid she might change her mind.

And the thought did occur to her, when he shoved off his trousers, and exposed the aggressive bulge of his arousal beneath the silk boxer shorts he still wore. He looked so big, so powerful, so dominant, as he loomed over her, that Jaime quivered. But then he bent his head to trace the line of her lips with his tongue, and her resistance simply faded away.

'Touch me,' he said, against her mouth, drawing her cold hands to his body. He insinuated her fingers into the waistband of his boxer shorts, and pushed himself against her, and Jaime's anxieties fled in a wave of shocked excitement.

He was hot and velvety to her touch, and he growled low in his throat when the pad of her thumb removed the pearl of moisture that glistened on his skin. His manhood throbbed with the needs she was arousing in him, and when he nudged her legs apart she guided him to her waiting source.

And it was like the first time for her. Philip had never entered her body so smoothly, so gently, pushing into her so fully that she was half afraid she would never be able to accommodate him. But she gave herself to Ben, allowing him to dictate what she could or could not do,

and the sensuous thrust of his body became a mindless
race for oblivion.

Jaime had never experienced anything like it. When
she married Philip, she had been a virgin, and his
treatment of her had left her convinced she would never
be able to sustain a normal relationship with any man.
But it wasn't true. Ben was proving it. As the pace of
his movements quickened, and the pulsing strength of
his manhood throbbed inside her, feelings that were
totally new to her began to spread to every fibre of her
being.

And, instead of remaining a passive participant in his
lovemaking, she found herself reaching for him,
clutching his shoulders, wrapping her legs around him,
as if she would never let him go. She couldn't get close
enough to him, and her fears now were that Ben would
leave her as empty and devastated as Philip had always
done.

Her breathing became heavy and laboured, an indication of the effort she was trying so desperately to hide,
and, as if sensing this, Ben lifted his head to look down
at her.

'Take it easy,' he said, smoothing the damp hair back
from her forehead with a slightly unsteady hand. 'You'll
make it,' he added. 'I'll see to that.'

'Will I?'

Jaime found her lips were dry, but when she tried to
moisten them Ben took her tongue between his teeth.
'Believe it,' he said, sliding his hand down between their
bodies to touch the pulsing nub of her femininity. 'Believe it,' he repeated, as she trembled beneath his stroking
fingers. 'Oh, God, you're so ready. Don't tell me you
don't feel it, too.'

Jaime's breathing felt suspended. Ben's probing fingers
had banished her fears and brought her to the very brink
of fulfilment. But, when he took his hand away again,
she almost cried out with frustration. Dear God, what
was he doing? she fretted wildly. Didn't he understand
how she was feeling?

And then, she realised that he did. When he moved
again, almost withdrawing from her body completely,
before burying himself in her again, awareness gripped

her. Now, when he moved, she moved with him, arching her back towards each thrust until wave after wave of unadulterated pleasure washed over her. It swept her up, and carried her higher and higher until the delight was so great that she was sure she couldn't bear any more.

Ben would have withdrawn from her then, but she wouldn't let him, she remembered unwillingly. He must have known, better than she did, the risks they were taking. But perhaps he had believed she was still taking some form of contraception, as she had all the time she was living with Philip. Whatever, seconds after she had achieved her climax, Ben had shuddered uncontrollably in her arms. He had spilled his seed inside her, and she could still feel its heat in her loins...

CHAPTER TEN

SO, THERE had been faults on both sides, she conceded now, sliding weary fingers through her hair. Ben had never intended their lovemaking to go as far as it had, and she had believed—foolishly, as it turned out—that he was making some kind of commitment. It hadn't been so.

Oh, he hadn't said as much that night. On the contrary, he had let her phone her parents and make up a story about their having dinner at some remote country hotel, and the car breaking down. And they had spent the rest of the night together.

Later, her mother had told her she hadn't believed her, but at the time her parents, like Ben, had thought she was old enough—and sensible enough—to take care of herself. Jaime shook her head. How wrong they had been!

It was weeks before she saw Ben again, weeks when she went through the whole gamut of emotions from dreamy contentment to disbelieving desperation. At first, she thought something must have happened to him, and she anxiously scanned every newspaper she could lay her hands on, in case she missed some small snippet of information about his whereabouts. But there was nothing to indicate why he hadn't contacted her again, and as the weeks passed, and the signs her body was giving her became unmistakable, disillusion set in.

Yet, even then, she had been prepared to give him the benefit of the doubt. When he appeared at the pub one lunchtime in early February, just as he used to do in the past, she had been pathetically eager to see him. But over lunch at the Crown he had dashed any lingering hopes she might have been nurturing. He had apologised—*apologised*—for what had happened at Christmas. It should never have happened, he said. He was a married man. *As if she didn't know that!* And he had no intention of leaving his wife.

Jaime told her parents the truth a few days later. She hadn't expected any sympathy, and she got none. She had behaved like a fool, for the second time in her life, and they had little patience with her. At first, her mother was outraged that she wasn't going to tell Ben that she was expecting a baby. He ought to know, she said. It was his child. The Russells could afford an extra mouth to feed. The Fenners couldn't. He should be made to pay for his pleasure.

It wasn't until Jaime explained her fears—that if Philip learned about the pregnancy, he might try to stop the divorce—that both her parents agreed she should go away to have the baby. A fictional lover was invented, someone Jaime had known before her marriage to Philip, and who might reasonably have come back on the scene now that she and her husband were separated. The story was helped along by the fact that Jaime went to stay with her father's sister in Newcastle. The Fenners let it be known that the young man in question came from there, and the gossips soon put it about that that was why Philip Russell was divorcing her. It was assumed that Jaime was the guilty party, and it was easier to allow her own name to be blackened than to defend something that was indefensible.

The only paradox was that Jaime never once thought of getting rid of the baby. However desperately she might deny it, she had wanted her baby, and she had been prepared to do anything to keep it. Even to the extent of keeping his identity a secret from any of the Russells. Tom was hers. He was her child. And when she learned that Ben had gone to live in South Africa, she had been sure she was safe from discovery...

Heaving a sigh, she propped her aching head in her hands. What time was it? she wondered. Heavens, it was late. Tom should be home by now. And she had to pull herself together before he saw her. It wouldn't do for him to get the wrong impression. Like imagining she was distressed because the man who had mercilessly abused her was dead, she acknowledged bitterly. God, leaving

Philip was the one sensible thing she had done in her life. No way was she going to let Tom believe otherwise.

But he might not see it that way, she realised uneasily. After the way he had reacted to Ben's appearance, the news that the man he believed was his father was dead was bound to come as something of a shock. It was possible that he had hoped that by associating with Ben he might get to meet him, too. She groaned. Was she never to be free of her youthful mistakes?

She shook her head. Ben should have told her the truth, right from the beginning, she thought, shifting at least part of the blame on to him. He had deliberately kept it from her for his own needs. He had known that without that lever she would never have allowed him to get near Tom.

She was pushing herself up from the table, when she heard the sound of Tom's key in the lock. For the first time since he was born she felt a sense of reluctance to confront him. What was she going to say? she fretted. How was she going to say it?

He came sauntering along the hall, whistling. He had seen the light in the kitchen, and guessed she was waiting for him. And, although she had never done it before, Jaime half wished she had gone to bed before he got home. She might have felt more equipped to deal with this in the morning.

But, as it happened, Tom looked more discomfited to see her than she was to see him. His attempted nonchalance faded at the sight of her taut expression, and she realised, in a flash, that he thought she was annoyed with him for being late.

'I can explain!' he exclaimed, before she could speak, and Jaime was tempted to let him go on thinking he was to blame. 'Angie's Dad asked me in for some supper, and—well, I couldn't say no, could I?'

'Are you sure it wasn't Angie who invited you in?' queried Jaime, and then, when her son began an indignant denial, she held up a calming hand. 'All right. All right. I believe you.' She paused, tried to compose her words, and then added, cowardly, 'So, you don't want a sandwich, or anything?'

'Well——' Tom shoved his hands into his trouser pockets, and hunched his shoulders '—I wouldn't say no.' He grimaced. 'I was offered lasagne, but I said I wasn't hungry.'

Jaime couldn't prevent a smile. 'Cheese all right?' she asked, turning to the fridge, and Tom nodded eagerly before straddling a chair at the table.

He looked so much like Ben, sitting there, watching her, that Jaime wondered anew how she could have fooled herself for so long. Was it simply a case of out of sight, out of mind, or had she actually deliberately blotted Ben's image from her memory?

'Did you have a nice evening?' he asked, gaining confidence from her attitude. 'What did you have to eat? Anything special?'

Jaime kept her eyes riveted on the bread she was buttering. 'Um—salmon mousse, and lamb,' she answered, without looking up at him. 'And—and an orange sorbet. It was delicious.'

Tom frowned. 'Was it?'

'Yes, of course.' Jaime did cast him a hasty look at that moment. 'Why do you ask? You know Mrs Haines is a good cook.'

Tom shrugged. 'You didn't have a row or anything?'

Jaime swallowed. 'Who?'

'You and Mrs Haines, of course.' Tom made a sound of impatience. 'Who else? There was only the two of you there!'

'No—ouch!' Jaime caught her thumb with the knife she was using to slice the cheese, and winced. 'I mean— there wasn't just the two of us there.' She hesitated. 'Ben Russell was there, too. And—and a doctor friend of Maggie's.'

'Uncle Ben was there?' Tom was staring at her now, and Jaime realised there was no going back. 'Did you know?'

'Did I know what?' Her son's words had diverted her, and Jaime gazed at him, confused. 'I don't understand.'

'Did you know he was going to be there?' exclaimed Tom irritably. 'Was that why you were so sure he wouldn't phone this evening?'

'No.' Jaime was getting impatient herself now. This was hard enough for her to say without Tom balking her at every turn. 'I had no idea he would be joining us until I got there. I wouldn't have gone if—well, I—might not have gone if—if——'

'If you'd known he was going to be there. Yes, I know.' Tom sounded fed up now. 'So, that's why you're looking so depressed.'

'I am not looking depressed!' Tom was getting the very impression she had hoped to avoid. 'Stop second-guessing my words. I've neither had a row——' liar! '—nor am I depressed. All right?'

Tom lifted his shoulders. 'If you say so.'

'I do say so.' Jaime set the cheese sandwich in front of him with scarcely concealed frustration. 'As a matter of fact—Ben—brought me home.'

'He did?' Tom was so surprised, the sandwich he had raised to his lips was forgotten. 'So what did he say? Did he mention my going over there this weekend?'

'No.' Jaime turned back to the breadboard, and brushed the crumbs she had made into the sink. 'He—well, he had some news for me, actually,' she admitted, setting the board in its place. And then, realising she was only making what she had to say that much more significant by prevaricating, she went on, 'He told me—Philip—is dead. Philip Russell, that is. Your—father.'

Tom put down the sandwich, untouched. 'He's dead?' he echoed, and Jaime nodded. 'How? When?'

'I—don't know the details.' Jaime guiltily acknowledged she should have asked. 'But—it was some time ago, I believe. He just didn't get around to telling us.'

Tom frowned. 'Dead,' he said again. And then, looking up, 'Were you upset?'

'No.' Jaime felt a deepening of colour in her cheeks, and wished she were not so susceptible to her emotions. 'No, Tom. I wasn't upset. My—relationship with Philip was not a happy one. I didn't wish him dead, but I can't pretend a sorrow I don't feel.'

Tom absorbed this in silence, and Jaime knew she had to say something more. She owed him that much. After all, Tom still believed that Philip Russell had been his father. How must he be feeling, hearing her condemn the man he believed had given him life?

'There's something else,' she said, coming to the table, and seating herself opposite him. 'Something I should have told you—ages ago. Only, it never seemed the right time.'

Tom looked at her warily, his eyes mirroring the uneasiness he was feeling. He was probably wondering what other awful revelations she was about to make, Jaime thought unhappily. And goodness knew, what she had to say wasn't going to be easy for either of them.

'It's about you,' she said slowly, understanding at last why adoptive parents were always advised to tell their children the truth as soon as they were old enough to understand. It was much harder to tell a boy of Tom's age that his father wasn't who he thought he was. 'Um—about your being born in Newcastle.'

'You mean, that story about you running away with another man is true?' exclaimed Tom gruffly, and Jaime gazed at him in disbelief.

'You know?'

'No.' Tom hunched his shoulders. 'I don't *know* anything. But I know the story. It's no secret, is it?'

'Isn't it?' Jaime felt as if someone had just delivered her a body blow. 'I—don't know what to say.'

'You were going to tell me about it,' Tom prompted flatly. 'It's true, then. Philip Russell wasn't my father.'

Jaime swallowed. 'No.'

'So—Uncle Ben isn't really my uncle?' This was evidently harder for him to say, and Jaime's heart went out to him.

'No,' she admitted huskily, wondering what he would say if she told him the truth. But she couldn't risk that. The Russells had taken so much from her. She couldn't risk losing her son to them as well, however selfish that might be.

'Does he know?'

Jaime blinked. She had been so wrapped up with her own thoughts that Tom's question caught her off guard. 'I beg your——?'

'Uncle—that is, Ben Russell. Does he know he's not my real uncle?'

'Oh.' Jaime licked her dry lips. 'I—yes. Yes, he knows——'

'He does?'

Tom's reaction was totally unexpected. The unhappy droop disappeared from his mouth like magic, and instead of regarding her with a mixture of hostility and accusation he looked positively delighted.

'He really knows?' he asked again, and when Jaime nodded, albeit a little less certainly now, Tom said, *'Yes!'* and raised both fists in a gesture of victory.

Jaime swallowed. 'You don't mind?'

'What about?' Tom picked up his sandwich, and, to his mother's astonishment, he bit into it. Then, with his mouth full, he went on, 'If you mean about Dad—that is, your ex-husband—I don't know how I feel. Not really. It's not as if I ever knew him, is it?'

'No, but——'

'I guess I always knew there had to be more to it than you had told me,' Tom went on, taking another bite of his sandwich. 'I mean, Dad—that is, *he*—divorced you, didn't he? I never could understand that until now.'

Jaime shook her head. In Tom's world, there were always absolutes. Philip had divorced her, therefore she *had* to be the guilty party. How could she explain that that had been one of the conditions Philip had demanded of Ben, when he agreed to stay away from her?

'You're not—angry, then?' she ventured, not quite knowing how to proceed, and after a moment Tom shook his head.

'Not angry, no. I wish you had told me sooner, that's all.' He paused. 'Did you—did you love him?'

'Who?' Jaime's mind refused to function. 'Oh—Philip! Well, I——'

'No. Not *him!*' exclaimed Tom, putting down his sandwich. His young face was flushed and awkward. 'I meant—my dad. My real dad.' He paused. 'Did you?'

'Oh!' Jaime expelled a noisy breath. She could see how important it was to him, and she realised she hadn't thought this through at all. The obvious progression hadn't even occurred to her. 'I—yes. Yes, I loved him.' She was glad she could be honest about that. 'But—

well, he was married. And, although I thought he intended to leave his wife, he didn't.'

Tom absorbed this silently. Then, picking up the
sandwich again, almost absently, she thought, he said,
'I suppose that's why you never talked about him.'

Jaime's lips tightened. 'Could be.'

Tom bent his head. 'Does—does he know about me?'

Oh, God! Jaime wondered how much more of this she
could take without screaming.

But, 'Yes,' she managed at last, waiting for the axe
to fall. It was only a matter of time before Tom asked
his name, and, in spite of all her misgivings, could she
honestly refuse to tell him?

'The bastard!' Tom's response, like his reaction to
Ben's knowing he wasn't Philip's son earlier, was the
exact opposite of what she had expected. 'He got you
pregnant, and then didn't even have the guts to do the
decent thing! Hell, Mum, how can you say you love
him?' He pushed his sandwich aside. 'I hate him!'

Jaime was speechless. His words shocked her so much
that the expletives he had used to make his point didn't
register until later. It wasn't until he flung back his chair
and got to his feet that she found her voice again.

'Where are you going?'

'Where do you think?' Tom was too upset to be polite.
'To bed, I suppose. What else is there?'

Jaime cleared her throat. 'Tom——' The words
wouldn't come, and she gazed at his stony face in helpless
confusion. 'Tom, about—about Ben...'

'Uncle Ben?' Tom's face softened. 'Oh, Mum, Uncle
Ben is the one good thing that's come out of all this.
Don't you see? When you said he knew I wasn't—wasn't
Philip Russell's son, I was so relieved!' He looked at
the ceiling for a moment, and Jaime's heart plummeted
when she saw the unfamiliar glint of tears in his blue
eyes. 'You see,' he added doggedly, 'it means he likes
me for who I am, not because he believes I'm his nephew.
I can still go on seeing him, can't I, Mum? Just because—just because that man's dead, it won't make any
difference, will it?'

                    *   *   *

She should have told him then. Jaime knew it. But how could she do it? she argued defensively. How could she tell him about Ben, and destroy his relationship with the one person he seemed to admire? All right. So it was to her advantage as well, but so what? Didn't the end justify the means? Didn't she have some right to protect herself? At least until he was old enough to understand?

Not for the first time since Ben had come to live in Kingsmere, Jaime did not have a good night's sleep. She tossed and turned for hours, reliving every minute of that conversation with her son. Even when exhaustion took its toll, her dreams were all like nightmares. If she wasn't confronting images of Philip, rearing up from his grave to pursue her, she was locked in some filthy prison cell, watching Ben take Tom away from her.

She knew the dreams were conscience-related. Even though she might tell herself that by keeping the truth from Tom she was protecting Ben as well, it would take some time to construct a convincing case. Until then, she would just have to live with it. Why pre-empt disaster, when it could look after itself?

Breakfast was an uneasy meal. For her part, Jaime was still not convinced the worst was over. Tom might yet wish to pursue the discussion about his father, and she spent her time rehearsing responses to a variety of questions.

But, in the event, her fears proved groundless. Tom's uneasiness apparently stemmed from doubts that she might change her mind about him seeing Ben again. He spent the time it took to ladle a huge plate of cornflakes into his mouth reassuring himself that his mother would have no objections if Ben invited him to the Priory again. He had evidently not given up hope that Ben might phone, and Jaime had to concede that she wouldn't stand in his way.

All the same, she didn't deny to herself that the circumstances had changed. Now that Tom knew that Philip had not been his father, he might want to discuss it with Ben. She just hoped Ben would remember his promises to her.

Saturday passed slowly. Maggie phoned in the afternoon to assure herself that her guest had arrived home safely the night before, and Jaime took the opportunity to offer a belated vote of thanks for the evening.

'Sorry if I was a bit offhand,' she murmured, accepting that Maggie's part in the proceedings had been innocent enough. 'Um—you must come here next time.'

Maggie agreed, and after a brief discussion of the evening Jaime managed to get off the phone without saying anything incriminating. But, it hadn't been easy pretending she and Ben had parted on friendly terms. Particularly as Maggie thought she had been instrumental in bringing them together. If she only knew, thought Jaime bitterly, marching along the hall and into the kitchen. If it weren't for Tom, she would have told her exactly what kind of man Ben was.

Tom came in as Jaime was slamming saucepans on to the drainer, and, putting down his squash kit, he regarded her worriedly. 'Did—er—did Uncle Ben phone?' he asked, his tone a mixture of dismay and anticipation, and Jaime gave him an ugly look.

'No,' she said, taking a certain amount of malicious pleasure from the disappointment that crossed his face as she dashed his hopes. 'And don't leave those dirty things there. The clothes basket is upstairs.'

Tom picked up his kit again. 'So, what's wrong?' he exclaimed. 'You were all right when I went out.'

'I'm all right now,' said Jaime shortly. Then, as compunction set in, she added, 'I'm just not in the best of moods, that's all. Don't mind me. I'll feel better when I've had a bath and something to eat. Beefburgers OK?'

Tom still looked doubtful, but he was not about to argue. 'Yes, fine,' he agreed, hovering uncertainly in the hall doorway. 'Er—no one came, while I was out, did they? Like—like Angie, for example?'

'No one came and no one called,' his mother assured him in controlled tones. 'Oh—except for Mrs Haines. She called.' She paused. 'Now, if you don't mind, I'll go for my bath.'

The phone rang again when Jaime was in the bath. Perfect, she thought grimly, when Tom answered it and called that it was Uncle Ben—for him. All day she had been expecting Ben to ring, and he hadn't. But, as soon as she was unavailable, he did. Dammit, it was as if he had extra-sensory perception.

So, she wasn't really surprised when, a few minutes later, Tom came tapping at the bathroom door. 'Mum!' he called. 'Uncle Ben wants to know if I can go and spend the day with him tomorrow.' He hesitated, and when she made no immediate answer he appended, 'Is that all right with you, Mum? Mum, is it?'

No, it's not, Jaime responded savagely, but only to herself. Turning Tom against her would solve nothing. 'I—suppose so,' she conceded, hearing the grudging note in her voice that she wasn't quite able to disguise. 'Tell him I'll drop you off in the morning. There's no need for him to come and fetch you.'

'Well, he says he will,' Tom protested, but Jaime was adamant.

'I'll take you,' she insisted, her voice rising in spite of herself. 'You've got your own way, Tom, so don't push it.'

'Oh, all right.' Now that he had her permission, Tom was not above allowing his real feelings to show. 'I'll tell him you're curious to see where he lives, shall I? I'm sure he wouldn't mind if you wanted to take a look around.'

'Don't you dare,' shouted Jaime angrily, but Tom was already bounding down the stairs again. The only re-assurance she had was that he was laughing.

CHAPTER ELEVEN

JAIME was gardening when Tom came home.

She had spent a lot of time in the garden during the past couple of weekends, expunging her frustration by dead-heading the roses, and pulling weeds. As luck would have it, there were plenty of weeds to pull at this time of the year, and Jaime knew her garden borders had never looked more well tended. Not that her heart was really in it. When Tom was out, she was constantly thinking about where he was, and whom he was with. Nevertheless, the occupation did keep her hands busy, even if her thoughts were still free to torment her.

She knew she ought to be grateful that Ben had apparently taken the hint as far as she was concerned. Although Tom had spent the last three Sundays at the Priory, Ben hadn't made any further attempts to see her, or to get her to join them. And if Tom had any doubts about the situation they were easily submerged by his desire to be with Ben. Even Angie had to take a back seat when his 'uncle' called, and it was this, as much as anything, that irritated Jaime.

It wouldn't be so bad if Tom didn't insist on talking about what he had done when he got home. When he used to go out with Angie, Jaime had had to practically squeeze every atom of information out of him, but with Ben he seemed incapable of keeping quiet. She had had to suffer all the nauseating details of Ben's purchase of two mares and a stallion, and of how Tom had had his first riding lesson. The news that Ben had said he was a natural horseman came as no surprise, but she wished Tom didn't always expect her to show the same interest in what he had done as he did.

Just occasionally Tom did say something that, in spite of herself, she couldn't ignore. Like when he mentioned, almost in passing, that Ben hadn't been able to go swimming that day because he'd had a stomach upset. With some careful probing, Jaime had ascertained that Ben had apparently had a pain in his stomach and had sweated a lot. But he'd said it was nothing serious, Tom had informed her, more intent on talking about how many lengths of the pool he had swum than worrying about something he regarded as unimportant, and Jaime had had to contain her anguish.

And, for the most part, she managed to hide her feelings. As far as Tom was concerned, she appeared to tolerate the time he spent with his uncle fairly well, and, although it took some swallowing, she knew her son had never been happier. Ben had given him what Jaime had never been able to: a man in his life, and Tom was content.

This afternoon, however, Jaime had had other thoughts on her mind. It was only a week now until Tom broke up for his summer holiday, and she couldn't help worrying about what Ben might have planned for the long vacation. It was obvious Tom would hope to spend more time at the Priory, once the demands of school had been removed, and, because she would be working, she would have no excuse to complain. As it was, she was sure Tom would spend every Saturday as well as every Sunday with Ben, if he had the chance. But, for reasons best known to himself, Ben never impinged on their Saturdays together, and on that day at least she could pretend that everything was still as it used to be.

But, of course, it wasn't. Tom could hardly string two sentences together without mentioning something to do with Ben, and the opportunities Ben was providing were giving her son a confidence he had never had before. Before her eyes he was developing, maturing, and it frightened her that he might guess the truth before she had a chance to tell him.

That was why, when she heard the front door slam, her heart skipped a couple of beats. A quick glance at her watch informed her that it was barely half-past three, and Tom had never been home earlier than seven o'clock before.

Peeling off her gardening gloves, she got up from the kneeler she was using, but before she could reach the back door Tom himself appeared. He slouched moodily against the door-jamb, his eyes averted from her half-enquiring, half-anxious stare, and Jaime was convinced now that something momentous had happened.

Ignoring the sick feeling in her stomach, she decided not to invite trouble by asking for it. Instead, she adopted what she hoped was a casual stance, and said brightly, 'You're early.'

'Mmm.'

Tom's response was in keeping with his brooding expression, and, folding the gardening gloves into a roll, Jaime thrust them into the pocket of her cotton dungarees. Then, walking purposefully towards him, she forced him to move aside.

'Um—I was just going to get myself a cool drink. Do you want one?'

'No, thanks.'

Tom swung round on the wood frame, and watched her as she took a can of Diet Coke from the fridge, and peeled off the tab. Jaime hoped he wasn't observing how her hands were shaking, or, if he did, that he assumed it was from tugging on the weeds. But the cool cola was invigorating, and she determinedly swallowed every mouthful before turning to face her son again.

And even then her heart went out to him. Whatever had happened, she could never blame him for it. This was all her fault, whatever she had said to Ben. She had made the mistakes, and she was going to have to pay for them.

Tom was still supporting his shoulders against the frame, his hands pushed into the pockets of his jeans. In the narrow-legged jeans and a navy-blue polo shirt he looked much younger than she had expected, and she bit her lip uncertainly, not quite knowing what to say.

But, in the event, Tom solved the problem for her. 'Don't you want to know why I've come home so early?' he asked, studying his canvas-booted foot as he scuffed it on the threshold. 'I know that's what you're thinking. I can see it in your face.'

Jaime took a deep breath. 'All right. Why are you home so early? I don't suppose—Ben threw you out, did he?'

'No.' Tom looked up, his expression indignant. 'No, I walked out.'

'Ah!' Jaime just managed not to groan. 'So—why did you walk out?'

'Because of *her*! Uncle Ben's mother! Mrs Russell!'

Jaime swallowed. 'Mrs Russell—was there?' she echoed faintly. 'Oh, God!'

'Yes. That's how I feel,' muttered Tom angrily. 'Ugly old cow! I hate her!'

'Tom!' Even in the midst of her despair, Jaime still found the strength to object to his language, but her son was not in a mood to placate her.

'I mean it,' he said, pushing away from the door, and stamping across the room. 'You don't know what she said. What she implied. I wanted to hit her. I wanted to jam my fist right into her fat, supercilious face!'

'Oh, Tom——'

'No. Don't try to defend her. I know you're going to say what you always say—that the Russells never approved of your marrying their son, but that's no reason for her to talk about you the way she did!' He sniffed. 'Especially not to me!'

Jaime shook her head. 'Tom——'

'She said some awful things,' Tom went on, disregarding her interruption. He obviously needed to talk it out of his system, and, however painful it might be, Jaime decided to let him. 'She said you'd only married—Philip—for his money. She said you'd never cared for him at all. Not really. You just wanted what he could give you.' He sniffed again, and raked agitated fingers through his silky hair. 'I said that wasn't true. That if it had been you'd have still been married to him. You wouldn't have fallen in love with my father, and given up a comfortable life in London for an uncomfortable one in Newcastle.'

Jaime caught her breath. 'Oh, Tom——'

'But she wouldn't listen,' he continued. 'She said it wasn't like that. That you wouldn't have left Philip if he hadn't found out that you'd been—making it with other men. He threw you out, that's what she said. As soon as he found out what you'd been doing, he washed his hands of you, and—and out of spite you lied to him, pretending I—I wasn't really his son!'

'Oh, God!'

Jaime dragged a chair out from the table and sank down into it. For a few seconds, she'd hoped for a miracle, she realised that now. When Tom first started speaking, she'd half believed it wasn't going to be as bad as she had anticipated. Tom was so loyal, so unwilling to believe anything bad of her that she'd really thought Mrs Russell had made a bad mistake.

But she was wrong. She had made the mistake. In her eagerness to see Tom's behaviour as a natural response to any attack on her integrity she'd forgotten one crucial point. She hadn't taken Tom's likeness to his grandfather into consideration. She'd completely overlooked Ben's reaction when he first set eyes on his son.

'So—am I *his* son?' Tom asked now, evidently misinterpreting her reactions, and Jaime looked up at him with anxious eyes.

'No,' she said steadily, wondering if she'd have been as honest if he'd asked if he was a Russell. 'No, you're not Philip's son, Tom. Whatever she says, it's not true.'

Tom's eyes were unnaturally bright, and Jaime realised how near to tears he was. The anger that had sustained him on his journey home was breaking down, and it infuriated her anew that he should be the innocent brunt of their mistakes.

'Tell me,' she said, realising she had to be strong enough for both of them, 'what did Ben—Uncle Ben—say about this? I—I assume he was there.'

'Part of the time,' Tom agreed gruffly. 'She—that is, Mrs Russell—arrived unexpectedly.' So, at least Ben hadn't arranged it, Jaime consoled herself grimly. 'We—we were planning on going riding. And then—she turned up.'

'Mr Russell wasn't with her.'

'No.' Tom shrugged. 'Just her.'

'Go on.'

'Well, she sort of—did a double-take, when she saw me. I didn't know who she was at first. Curtis—that's Uncle Ben's houseman—he let her in. I guess he assumed it wasn't necessary to announce her.'

'I see.' Jaime's throat was dry.

'Uncle Ben looked a bit sick, too,' Tom continued. 'I think he wasn't too pleased about her not phoning to let him know she was coming.' He paused. 'Anyway, as I say, she was pretty shocked to see me. She asked Uncle Ben who I was in a kind of squeaky voice, and when he told her she sort of staggered to a chair and sat down. I guess I must look a bit like Philip or something, because she definitely saw a likeness. Actually, that was how Uncle Ben came to leave us alone. She asked him if he'd get her a drink. I don't think he was too keen, but she did look a bit pale, so he didn't have much choice.'

'And that was when she—she spoke to you?'

Tom nodded. 'As soon as Uncle Ben went out, she asked me how old I was.'

'And you told her?'

'Yes.' Tom looked indignant. 'Why shouldn't I?'

'No reason.' Jaime's voice was a little defensive, too. 'Carry on.'

'There's not much more to say.' Tom hunched his shoulders. 'As soon as she heard how old I was, she started on about you. She said you were an evil woman. That you'd spread lies about my father——'

'Philip wasn't your father!'

'No. Well, I'm only telling it the way it was,' exclaimed Tom tremulously. 'It was awful, Mum, honestly. Like a nightmare. She was shouting her head off when Uncle Ben came back.'

Jaime caught her lower lip between her teeth. 'And— and what did he say?'

'He told her to shut up.' A spasm of emotion feathered his flesh. 'He said I shouldn't listen to her, and that she was just a bitter old woman. And—and then she turned on him. Just like that. Telling him he was a fool if he believed anything you said. I—I just wanted to get away.'

His shoulders were shaking now, and, leaping up from her chair, Jaime put her arms about him. It was years since Tom had allowed any overt affection from her, but this time he didn't try to draw away. Instead, the tears he had been holding back began streaming down his cheeks, and Jaime's fury was fuelled by his innocent frustration.

When he was able to speak again, he mumbled, 'Uncle Ben didn't bring me home, you know,' and Jaime drew back to look at him.

'He didn't?' In spite of her insistence that Tom could just as easily take a bus home from the Priory, Ben invariably dropped him off. 'Why not?'

'Because I didn't want him to,' declared Tom forcefully, scrubbing a resentful hand across his eyes. It was obvious he was beginning to regret having broken down like that, and Jaime's throat felt tight with suppressed emotion. 'I don't want to see either him or his mother again,' he added, marching into the hall. 'You were right, Mum. We don't need him. He'd just better bloody well keep away!'

Ben rang at five o'clock. Jaime had been expecting him to appear in person, firmly convinced that he wouldn't allow his mother to come between him and his own son, whatever Tom might have to say about it. But, as usual, he did the unexpected.

'Is he home?' he asked without preamble as soon as Jaime had given the number.

Her involuntary, 'Of course,' seemed to satisfy him.

'Good,' he said flatly, making no attempt to apologise for what had happened. 'Tell him I rang, will you?' And put the receiver down again before Jaime could voice any kind of protest.

Of course, as soon as the phone went dead Jaime thought of a dozen things she should have said, but it was too late then. Besides, when she heard the betraying squeak of a floorboard on the landing she was glad she hadn't launched into some reckless tirade that could easily have got out of hand. Tom had heard enough for one day. But, just to keep the record straight, she did go upstairs and give him Ben's message.

'So what?' Tom countered from where he was sprawled on his bed looking at a magazine. Just as if he hadn't been crouched on the landing minutes before, thought Jaime cynically.

'He asked me to tell you, that's all,' she said, not really knowing why she had felt such a compulsion to do so.

'Well, I don't want to know,' muttered Tom, rolling on to his side away from her. 'I think I'll go and see Angie later. It doesn't matter to her who my father was.'

Felix remarked on the dark rings around Jaime's eyes the following morning, but she managed to evade any more searching questions. It did cross her mind to wonder if he had seen Maggie recently, and whether she had revealed the identity of two of her dinner guests, but happily that wasn't mentioned. If Felix knew she had seen Ben, he was keeping it to himself, and she could only be grateful.

But her fragile complacency took a decided dent midmorning, when Ben himself walked into the office. He strode into the reception area of the main office as Jaime was sharing her coffee-break with some of the other women, and her heart flipped a beat as his green gaze roved swiftly around the room.

Of course, his arrival caused a minor stir. His face was still familiar enough from the jackets of his books, and a few of the women were old enough to remember his television appearances. One or two of them even recalled the fact that Jaime had been married to his brother, and an awkward flush stained her cheeks as their eyes turned in her direction.

'Can I help you?'

Sharon Burrows, the youngest receptionist, was quick to offer her assistance, and Ben withdrew his gaze from Jaime's hot face long enough to give the girl a disarming smile.

'I just wanted a word with Mrs Russell,' he said, pushing his hands into the pockets of the worn denims he was wearing. When he smiled, the lines around his eyes disappeared, and Jaime guessed she was the only one who noticed how brittle that smile was.

But then, she was the only one who really knew him, she thought, acknowledging for the first time that their association had gone way beyond the bounds of a casual relationship. She might not like to admit it, but it was true. They had shared too much together to ignore it.

And his appearance worried her. Although she might resent the fact of his coming here, and involving her in a lot of unnecessary explanations, she couldn't deny that his gaunt face and hollow eyes disturbed her. Why hadn't Tom said anything? she wondered, and then realised that a boy of Tom's age was too young to notice any minor deterioration in his uncle's condition. And it was over three weeks since Jaime had seen him. Over three weeks since the night he had told her that Philip was dead.

'I—it's all right, Sharon. Mr Russell and I know one another,' she said now, coming forward. She schooled her features into a mask of politeness. 'Hello, Ben. This is a surprise.'

'Is it?'

Ben's response was hardly encouraging, and several of the women exchanged knowing glances. Jaime could guess what the gossip would be when they left the room, and, in spite of her anxieties about him, her lips tightened.

'Um—we can talk in my office,' she said, indicating the door into the corridor behind him, and without another word Ben turned and led the way out of the room. He didn't allow her to precede him. He merely held the door cursorily for her to pass through. But when the door had swung shut behind them, and they were alone in the corridor, he made no move to follow her into the adjoining office.

'I think—I think we should talk some place else,' he said, his voice clipped and monotonic, and Jaime caught her breath.

'I can't do that!'

'Why not?'

'You know why not. I—I have a job to do. You should have waited until—until lunchtime.'

'And risk you spending your lunch-hour here?' he exclaimed, taking one hand out of his pocket, and rubbing it against his thigh. 'Jaime, we have to talk. Now. I just don't think this is the place, that's all.'

Jaime glanced uneasily about her. 'What do you want me to do?' she demanded in an undertone. 'Tell Felix you're here? Let him know we have some private business to discuss? Do you want to broadcast this to the whole of Kingsmere?'

'I don't particularly care,' retorted Ben harshly. 'If we stay here, will that prevent him from finding out what's going on?'

Jaime sighed. 'You shouldn't have come!'

'No, I know. You've made that pretty clear. But unlike you I need some reassurance. For pity's sake, can't you understand that? I've been nearly out of my skull!'

Jaime took a steadying breath. 'All right.' Although what she had to say would take very little time, she found she couldn't just turn him away. She needed to know what was wrong with him. She needed to know what he was going to do now. 'Give me a minute.'

Felix was in conference with a client, which made it a little easier. It enabled her just to leave a note on her desk, informing him that she had had to go out for a while. She apologised for her absence, and added that she would explain when she got back. She just hoped she would be able to think of a satisfactory explanation for him. Somehow she knew he would hear about Ben's involvement before very long.

The Mercedes was parked outside, and this time a white parking ticket was tucked under the windscreen-wipers. Jaime expected Ben to say something, maybe mutter a curse or two, but he didn't. He just tugged the sheet of paper from beneath the rubber, screwed it up into a ball, and tossed it into the back of the car.

The negligence of this action brought an unwilling smile to Jaime's lips. Her reaction to one of those tickets would have been so different. She could imagine the sinking feeling she would have had in the pit of her stomach, the guilt she would have felt at breaking the law—not to mention the dismay at having to pay the fine. To Ben it was simply a minor irritation. The hardest part was tugging it off and screwing it up.

'This strikes you as amusing, does it?' Ben enquired now, jerking open his door, and joining her inside. His green eyes glittered. 'I guess you think you've won, don't you?'

Jaime gave him a startled look. 'No——'

'Then what's so funny?'

'You—throwing that parking ticket away,' muttered Jaime helplessly. 'For heaven's sake, Ben, I don't think what happened to Tom yesterday was at all funny. And nor would you if you'd seen him when he got home.'

Ben jammed the car into drive, and achieved the impossible. The superb gearbox showed its protest at such cavalier treatment by stalling, and they lurched to a halt.

'Sorry,' he mumbled, releasing the handbrake this time so that the big car could glide forward. 'I'm not in the best of tempers today.'

'Nor health, either,' commented Jaime, giving him a studied sideways glance. 'Are you still going to insist it's just a bug?'

'It is.' Ben was impatient, concentrating his attention on the traffic. 'I'm all right. I just didn't sleep very well last night, that's all.'

Jaime shook her head. 'I wish you'd be honest with me.'

'As you are with me, you mean?' he countered, swearing as a huge truck swung across his path. 'Forget about me, Jaime. It's Tom I'm concerned about.'

'Do you think I'm not?'

'No.' Ben gave her the compliment of believing her. 'But you hold all the cards at the moment. I—well, my position is—unnatural, to say the least.'

'Whose fault is that?'

'Not mine!' Ben was savage. 'God, I didn't even know you were pregnant, did I? You should have told me.'

'And then what would you have done? Left Maura? I don't think so. You'd already told me that wasn't going to happen.'

'OK, OK. We'll leave that for the moment.' Ben expelled his breath on a heavy sigh. 'But you must see what it's like for me now. God, you don't know how hard it was to stay away last night!'

Jaime pressed her lips together. 'Didn't your mother keep you company?' she asked rather maliciously, and Ben gave her a bitter look.

'That hardly deserves an answer,' he said. 'But since you ask, she left soon after Tom.'

Jaime bent her head. 'I expect it was quite a shock for her, too,' she said, trying to be charitable. 'Does she know everything?'

Ben's lips twisted. 'I didn't tell her, if that's what you're asking. But pride, frustration—call it what you will—did enable me to convince her that Tom isn't Philip's son.'

Jaime glanced at him. 'And she believed you?'

'After she'd been apprised of some of the least attractive facets of your marriage—yes, I think so.'

Jaime's hands curled together in her lap. 'You *told* her?'

'What she hadn't already guessed,' said Ben wearily. 'Jaime, what kind of a life do you think Phil's been living all these years? Yours wasn't the only unpleasantness they—my parents—have had to swallow. You didn't ask how Phil died, but I'll tell you anyway. It was in the apartment of a known homosexual. They'd been experimenting with some new substance. According to the post-mortem, Phil had enough cocaine in his bloodstream to kill him several times over.'

'Oh, God!'

Jaime felt sick. She had never dreamt Philip's death had been anything other than natural. A heart attack, perhaps, or some fatal illness. But instead...

Ben seemed to realise something was wrong when she said nothing more, and after a swift look in her direction he sighed. 'I'm sorry,' he said. 'I suppose I shouldn't have blurted it out like that, but you deserve to know the truth.'

Jaime was trembling. 'Thank God—thank God he wasn't Tom's father,' she muttered, turning her face away, and Ben's hands gripped the steering-wheel just a little bit tighter.

CHAPTER TWELVE

IT WASN'T until Ben slowed, before turning the big car through tall iron gates, that Jaime realised where they were. She had been so shocked by what he had told her that she hadn't been paying attention to her whereabouts, but now she sat up straight and looked accusingly at him.

'What do you think you're doing?' she exclaimed. She jerked back the cuff of her cream blouse and stared disbelievingly at her watch. 'I should have been back in the office five minutes ago!'

Ben gave her a tired stare. 'We haven't talked yet,' he reminded her. 'Not about Tom, anyway.'

'Then it'll have to wait——'

'*No!*' He fairly ground out the word. 'Stop it, Jaime. We are going to talk, and if it means Haines chucks you out then so be it. I'll see you don't starve!'

Jaime's face contorted. 'You'll give me money, is that what you're saying? Oh, that's typical! You think money solves everything, don't you? Money and possessions! Well, they don't! It's people who matter—nothing else!'

Ben allowed her to go on, but he didn't attempt to answer her. Instead, he brought the car to a precise stop at the foot of the steps leading up to the Priory's double doors, and turned off the engine.

'I won't get out,' said Jaime childishly as he thrust open his door, and his face twisted in a slight smile.

'You will,' he promised her, withdrawing the keys from the ignition and pocketing them just in case. He slammed his door, walked round the bonnet, and opened hers. 'Do it! Now!'

'No.'

Jaime looked up at him defiantly, finding her second wind in thwarting him like this. If he wanted her out, he'd have to lift her off the seat. And looking at him just now, he didn't appear to have the strength to do so.

But she was wrong. The hand that fastened around her arm had more than enough power to jerk her out of the Mercedes, and even when she was standing beside him on the tiled forecourt he didn't release her.

'Let's go,' he said, after slamming the car door, and, although Jaime resented his arrogance, the appearance of another man in the Priory entrance momentarily kept her silent. He was a huge man, thick-set and completely bald, and she guessed this must be the houseman Tom had mentioned. 'Meet Curtis,' added Ben, in unknowing confirmation, and Jaime summoned up a polite smile of acknowledgement. 'This is Mrs Russell, Curtis. Tom's mother.'

'Delighted to meet you, Mrs Russell.'

Curtis's refined voice was in direct contrast to his bruising appearance, and Jaime exchanged a startled look with Ben before returning the greeting.

'We'll have some coffee in the library, Curtis,' Ben ordered as the man stepped aside to allow them to precede him into the building. 'As soon as you can.'

'Yes, sir.'

Curtis followed them into the huge vaulted entrance hall, closing the twin doors with practised ease. But Jaime only noticed that in passing. Her attention was caught by the skill with which the cold austerity of the hall had been transformed. It was common knowledge that in Sir Peter Dunstan's day the Priory had not been the most comfortable of residences. Little money had been spent on restoration, and Jaime remembered that Philip had once commented on how poorly heated it had been.

Now the flags, which had once been so cold to walk on, had been replaced by a mosaic of marble tiles, and the stone walls had been panelled with a rich, mellow wood. The huge fireplace hadn't been replaced, but the stonework had all been cleaned and polished, and an assortment of fire-irons did not look out of place, arranged in a fan-shaped semi-circle inside a shining brass urn.

'It's this way.'

Ben's hand in the small of her back nudged her forward, and she went with him almost without thinking, still absorbed in admiring her surroundings. There were windows set high up in the walls, modern stained-glass windows, whose leaded panes cast the light in shades of blue and green and yellow. It was a clever device to retain the fundamental feeling of the priory, and within its thick walls it was possible to sense a little of the peace and sanctuary its original occupants had sought.

They left the hall through an arched doorway, and entered a panelled corridor, with a beautifully restored wooden staircase mounting to their left. As Tom had described in such eager detail, several rooms opened from the corridor, and through open doorways Jaime glimpsed other rooms, leading one from another. She had a swift impression of lovingly polished wood and leather, tall cabinets and squashy sofas, acres of exotically woven carpets, and rich velvet drapes in jewel-bright colours.

Then Ben opened a leather-studded door to their right, and Jaime found herself in the library. But it was obvious it wasn't just a reading-room. A huge square desk was set beneath the long leaded windows, and the rather incongruous sight of a computer completed her belief that this was probably where Ben did most of his work. It also reminded her of the fact that this was the first time she had visited some place that actually belonged to him. In the past, he had always come to see her—first at the pub, and then, latterly, at the house in Dorset Road. Still, he could hardly have invited her to his home when Maura was alive, she reflected tensely, and with that thought came the reminder of why she was here.

Ben propelled her into the room, and then closed the door and leaned back against it. 'Sit down.'

Jaime held up her head. 'I'd rather not.'

'Oh, for God's sake, can't we stop this childishness? All right. Perhaps I shouldn't have implied that you're not indispensable to Haines, but, for pity's sake, does it matter? In the present circumstances, does anything matter?'

Jaime drew an uneven breath. 'I rather thought that was why I was here.'

Ben's mouth compressed. 'All right. So that's another point to you. Now, can we talk about Tom?'

Jaime bent her head. 'You hurt him.'

'*I* didn't hurt him.' Ben was indignant. 'I didn't know my mother was going to turn up like that.'

'But you left her alone with him,' accused Jaime, looking at him again. 'You let her tear me to shreds——'

'No——'

'Yes!'

The knock at the door came as something of a relief to both of them, and Ben wearily moved aside to let Curtis into the room. The houseman set the tray containing a bone china jug of coffee, two cups, cream and sugar on a low table, near a screened fireplace. Then, straightening, he asked if Mrs Russell would be staying to lunch.

Jaime was about to say no, when Ben beat her to it. 'I think not,' he said, his lips pulled into an ironic line. 'But no calls, Curtis. Not unless you think it's urgent. And—thanks.'

'Yes, sir.'

Curtis allowed Jaime a slight lifting of his lips before withdrawing from the room. After he had closed the door again, Ben gestured towards the hearth, and the two dark green velvet sofas that faced one another across the coffee-table.

'Truce? At least while we drink our coffee?'

Jaime hesitated. 'I ought to be going.'

Ben sighed. 'But you're not.'

'Do you intend to keep me here by force?'

'Don't talk rubbish!' Ben was supporting himself now, with the back of one of the sofas, and, realising he needed to sit down probably more than she did, Jaime gave in. But she took the sofa opposite, perching on the edge of the cushions, as if, by not relaxing, she could keep some control of the situation.

'OK.' Without waiting for her to take charge of the tray, Ben slumped into his seat, and poured the coffee himself. He added cream but no sugar to Jaime's, and then pushed the cup towards her. 'When can I see Tom?'

'How did you know I take cream but no sugar?' countered Jaime, without answering him, and Ben ran a frustrated hand over his hair.

'It's the way you had it at Maggie's,' he answered, making no attempt to touch the coffee he had poured for himself. 'Jaime, when can I see Tom? I can't wait until next weekend. I have to talk to him.'

'Well, he doesn't want to talk to you,' retorted Jaime, sipping from her own cup. She held it between her hands so that it wouldn't clatter in its saucer. But her eyes darted away from his, and the look of stunned disbelief she saw there.

'What do you mean, he doesn't want to talk to me?' Ben was bewildered. 'Did he say that?'

'Of course.' Jaime was indignant now. 'I haven't stopped you from seeing him before, have I?'

'Moot point,' said Ben flatly, resting his forearms along his spread legs, and gazing down at the rug at his feet. 'I don't believe it.'

'What don't you believe?' Jaime put down her cup. 'I'm not lying——'

'I'm not saying you are.' Ben's eyes when he looked at her now were dull and heavy-lidded. 'I just don't believe the relationship Tom and I have built up over the past few weeks can be destroyed by my mother's malice.'

Jaime shrugged. 'I'm sorry.'

'So what did he say?'

Jaime lifted her shoulders. Despite their lustreless appearance, Ben's eyes were still disturbingly intent. 'I—what about?' she asked evasively. 'I've told you. Tom doesn't want to see—any of you again.'

'Which means he doesn't want to see his grandmother again,' declared Ben tersely. 'Don't worry. He won't.'

'No.' Jaime was quick to disabuse him. 'That's not what he meant. I don't think he wants to come here again.'

'Did he say that?'

'Not in so many words, perhaps,' admitted Jaime honestly. 'But you must know how he was feeling when he left here yesterday afternoon. For heaven's sake, he wouldn't even let you bring him home!'

Ben sagged back against the cushions. He closed his eyes, and Jaime's heart turned over. He looked awful. More drawn than he had looked when he came to the office, and in spite of herself she couldn't deny the surge of concern that swept over her. Whatever else, she had loved him—once. Tom was his son, and some bonds were impossible to break.

'Ben?' she ventured anxiously, and when he didn't answer her she left her seat. She circled the table, and bent over him, briefly brushing her hand against his temple. His skin was hot, yet both damp and feverish. It was obvious he was still suffering the effects of some infection, and she wished there was something she could do to alleviate his pain.

And then, as she was withdrawing her hand, his eyes opened. His action startled her, as much because she had half believed he was unaware of her nearness as by the sudden clarity of his vision. She had thought he was too drained, both physically and emotionally, to care whether or not she touched him. But he lifted his hand and captured her wrist with forceful fingers.

'What the hell do you think you're doing?'

Jaime gulped. 'Well, I wasn't about to strangle you, if that's what you're afraid of,' she retorted, taking refuge in sarcasm, but he didn't let her go.

'Do you care about me, Jaime?' he asked wonderingly, startling her afresh, and she was still searching for an answer when he pulled her hand against his mouth. His lips brushed her knuckles with delicate sensuality, and then he turned her palm against his tongue.

Jaime's knees shook. 'I—of course I'd care about anyone in your condition——' she began, trying to draw her hand away.

'That's not what I asked,' Ben interrupted, looking up at her through the thick veil of his lashes. 'I asked if you cared about *me*.' He took the tip of her forefinger between his teeth. 'There is a subtle difference.'

'Not—not to me.' Jaime could feel a feathering of perspiration on her back and beneath her breasts. 'Ben, this isn't getting us anywhere.'

'I disagree.' His pallor was giving way to a hectic flush of colour, investing him with an unnatural look of health.

'You do care, don't you?' His lips twisted. 'Don't deny it.'

'Ben——'

'It's hell, isn't it?' he muttered, and before she realised what he intended to do he had jerked her down on top of him.

He sucked in his breath as her weight almost knocked the air out of him. But it was only a momentary weakness. As she struggled to find her feet, he took advantage of her flailing legs to roll her over on to her back, then the solid length of his body provided more than an adequate restraint. His chest crushed her breasts. The buckle of his belt dug into her waist. And his legs meshed with hers, sending her skirt riding up her thighs.

But it was the nearness of his mouth that troubled her most. Hot breath fanned her cheek, and the roughness of his jaw scraped her chin. He was breathing as fast as she was, faster, as he levered himself above her, capturing her face between his hands, and lowering his lips to hers.

His kiss was fierce, demanding, burning with a hunger she tried to tell herself was fuelled by his frustration over Tom. But, as always when he touched her, coherent thought became a problem. Her mind swam. Images of the past—of Maura, and of Tom—became just a hazy memory. When he moved against her, when the thrusting urgency of his arousal became a palpable pressure on her stomach, she could no longer rationalise his need away. He wanted *her*! Not her sympathy, but her body, and, crazy as it was, she couldn't find the strength to stop him.

'God—Jaime,' he gasped, releasing her mouth to find the pulse that raced below her ear. His tongue probed the fluttering beat, dewing it as he tasted her skin, drawing a laboured breath.

Her breathing became quick and shallow. Beside her, on the sofa, her hands opened and closed convulsively. She wanted to touch him. She wanted to slide her hand between them, and feel the throbbing heat that swelled against her. A little moan escaped her, as his fingers probed the chaste neckline of her blouse to caress her quivering flesh, and when he tugged the buttons from their holes she could resist no longer.

'Don't stop me,' he muttered, as she lifted her hands, but Jaime didn't even want to try. His mouth had covered hers again, and his tongue was sliding between her lips, making any kind of resistance impossible.

Besides, Jaime didn't want to resist. Ben's shirt was open at the neck, and her hands were already exploring the smooth skin of his shoulders. Touching him, caressing him, feeling the instinctive response of his flesh as he thrust himself against her, Jaime was beyond thinking of anything but him. She had forgotten where she was. She had forgotten that Ben had servants who could appear at any time. Even when he pushed her skirt above her hips, and hooked his fingers into the waistband of her bikini pants, she didn't object. And when his hand closed possessively over the cluster of blonde curls at the junction of her legs she arched helplessly against him.

'Do you like that?' he demanded unsteadily, lifting his head to look down at her, and she nodded helplessly. 'So sweet,' he muttered, transferring his gaze to where his fingers rubbed against a tingling nub of flesh. 'I want to feel you—against me,' he added hoarsely. 'Oh, God, Jaime, I love you. And I want you. Now. This minute. Help me!'

And she did. Even though the fact that they were still practically fully dressed ought to have deterred her, it didn't. She wanted to feel his turgid flesh against her and in her just as much as he did, and she couldn't wait any longer either.

Ben unfastened his belt with unsteady fingers, while Jaime dealt with his zip. Then, supporting himself on one hand, he thrust his jeans and the black silk boxer shorts he wore beneath down to his knees. But it wasn't far enough and, with a groan, he kicked them down to his ankles. Then, parting her legs, he eased himself into her, and Jaime's flesh closed about him in fervent anticipation.

'Oh, God! Ben...'

Jaime's world tilted at the infinite delight of having him inside her, expanding her, swelling her, filling her, sending all her senses reeling. His hands curled about her buttocks, lifting her even closer, and her legs coiled eagerly about his hips.

It was a reckless loving, Jaime realised afterwards. Neither of them had taken any precautions against the possible consequences of their actions, but just then such details seemed of little significance. All that was important was the fact that by some miracle they were together again, and the urgent needs of mind and body far surpassed any rational thought.

For Jaime, it was as if time had slipped and she was a girl again, experiencing her first real taste of sensuality at Ben's hands. She had never forgotten the gentleness he had showed her then, or the eager passion that had flowered from those first moments of sweetness. She had wanted him then, and she wanted him now, and she would face the whys and wherefores of that situation later. Right now, all that mattered was that he wanted her, too, and when his parted lips sought hers again she thrust her tongue into his mouth.

The crescendo was building, slowly at first, but ever more rapidly, as Ben withdrew, only to bury himself even more deeply inside her. He was sweating, they were both sweating, the moist heat of their bodies welding them together in an urgent cocoon of passion.

Ben wasn't being gentle with her now. Gentleness had given way to raw male need, but Jaime gloried in it. She wasn't afraid of Ben. She had never been afraid of Ben. Whatever he asked, she gave, willingly. She submerged herself in his needs, his hungers, and in so doing found her own salvation.

She became as demanding as he was, touching him as he was touching her, doing things she knew instinctively would please him. With eyes open, and blazing with the emotions he had ignited, she thrust herself against him, making little sounds of pleasure as he opened her shirt and caressed her breasts.

She felt as if she was on fire. Her body had become some unfamiliar, mindless entity that she could no longer control. She gave it into his keeping, with no thought for tomorrow, trusting him implicitly, abandoned to whatever fate had in store.

And the climax came, as wild and untrammelled as their loving. Ben reared above her, watching her as she reached the final peak of understanding, looking down at the place where their bodies were joined with eyes dark with his own unguarded passion. Then he too threw back his head in anguish, shuddering to his own release, before slumping heavily on top of her.

It was several minutes before Jaime became aware of ordinary things again. And then it was the steady ticking of the clock on the marble mantelshelf that brought an unwilling return of sanity. Its measured beat was an echo of the dull throbbing in her chest which was so much slower now that her brain was functioning again. Of course, that awareness alone brought a slight oscillation in her heart's rhythm, but she forced down her panic, and set about trying to extricate herself from her position.

It wasn't easy. Ben was still wrapped around her, and the sticky aftermath of sex made any kind of withdrawal a problem. But the voices inside her head wouldn't let her just lie there and enjoy it. No matter that minutes before she had wanted to get under his skin. Right now, the loudest voices were those of scorn and accusation, and the images she could see behind her eyes made instant movement a necessity.

Dear God, she thought, pressing the heels of her hands against his shoulders, what if Curtis should open the door and find them like this? Of course, it was possible that he was not unused to finding his employer in positions that could at best be called compromising, but she was not that kind of woman. She didn't care if Ben made love on his sofa every day of the week; she didn't.

Of course, that wasn't true either. She did care, badly, but that was something she would have to deal with in some other place at some other time. It was not something she intended to share with Ben. Not when she had just made the second big mistake of her life.

'Relax,' he mumbled now, as she tried to wriggle away from him, and tears stung the backs of her eyes at the realisation that Ben probably thought he had the upper hand now.

'I—want to get up,' she said, aware of how impossible that was going to be without his co-operation. 'Please.' The polite request almost choked her. 'Someone might come in.'

'That didn't seem to bother you before,' remarked Ben drily, the faint abrasion of his beard making her wince. Her jaw felt sore, and she pressed her lips together at this further proof of his possession of her.

'Nevertheless——'

'OK.' With a groan of submission, Ben rolled over on to his back, and Jaime took the opportunity to scramble hastily to her feet.

But the ignominy of having to repair her clothing in front of him brought a flush of colour to her face, and she turned her back as she refastened her bra and cobbled together the buttons of her blouse.

'Don't forget these,' murmured Ben mockingly, and she turned to find a lazy scrap of cotton dangling from his finger. It was her bikini pants, and she snatched them out of his hand. But she didn't put them on. Not then. She thrust them into her pocket, and Ben raised his eyebrows in teasing disbelief.

'Why don't you cover yourself?' she exclaimed hotly, embarrassed beyond bearing by his cool appraisal, and, with a sigh, Ben levered himself up on his elbows.

'I suppose I should,' he observed lazily, but he didn't make any move to do so, and Jaime's eyes were irresistibly drawn to the male beauty of his body.

'Oh, for goodness' sake!' she floundered, turning away. 'You're impossible!'

'Don't you mean incredible?' he teased huskily, but she only hunched her shoulders, hardly aware of him making himself decent, until his hands descended on her shoulders and he turned her to face him. 'There. Will that do?'

He had pulled up his pants, but his belt and his shirt still hung loose on his lean body. In spite of herself, Jaime was helplessly aware of him, and of the musky smell of their lovemaking that pervaded the air. But she had to steel herself against any more mistakes, and when she turned her head away and her eyes alighted on the clock she didn't have to pretend her dismay.

'It's nearly twelve o'clock!' she cried, staring at the hands of the brass carriage clock as if transfixed. 'Good God, Felix will be furious!'

'To hell with Felix!' said Ben harshly. 'You and me—we're more important than Felix Haines!'

'Don't you mean—you and *Tom*?' demanded Jaime scornfully. 'Don't think I don't understand what all this was about. If you couldn't get to Tom one way, you thought you could get to him another. I'm not a fool!'

Ben's hands dropped to his sides, and he stepped back, his face a stunned mask. 'You don't believe that!'

'Don't I?' Jaime didn't know what she believed any more. 'All I know is, you brought me here for some purpose——'

'Yes. To talk!'

'But we didn't do a lot of talking, did we?' Jaime was trembling from head to toe. 'You—you tricked me into feeling sorry for you, and then—and then you did what you knew had seduced me before, and which you thought would seduce me again. Well, you were wrong. The sex was good, but it hasn't changed my mind about a thing. Do what you like. I'm going back to work!'

Jaime had a blinding headache by the time she got home that evening. She told herself it was because she had had to work twice as hard that afternoon, to make up for the time she had lost in the morning, but it wasn't that. Even though Felix had forborne from asking where she had been, she was still devastated over what had happened at the Priory, and no matter how she tried to avoid it she knew she had only herself to blame.

But it wasn't just the sense of responsibility she felt for what had happened that was troubling her. If she could have accepted the blame and dismissed it, she might have been able to live with herself. But she couldn't. She kept seeing Ben's face, when she had accused him of tricking her, and experiencing again the anxiety she had felt when he had lurched across the room and yelled for Curtis. He hadn't seemed to care that his appearance alone must have been a blatant advertisement of what had happened. He had just hung weakly against the door, as he'd issued his orders for Curtis to take her back to her office, and the sound of the library door slamming behind her had rung in her ears for hours.

In consequence, she was in no mood to humour her son. Tom was waiting for her when she got home, and he was gruff and resentful, obviously suffering his own misgivings for what had happened the day before.

'You're late,' he said, by way of a greeting, and it took all Jaime's self-control not to turn on him, too. She could have accused him of laziness, of not making any contribution to the meal he objected having to wait for, but she didn't. She had enough on her conscience, she thought miserably. Dear God, what was going to happen now?

The doorbell rang as she was trying to swallow a mouthful of baked potato, and she turned anxious eyes in Tom's direction. 'Angie?'

'I doubt it.' Tom shovelled another forkful of beans into his mouth, and shrugged his shoulders indifferently. It was obvious his appetite had not been affected by his feelings, and, realising he had no intention of answering the door, Jaime got wearily to her feet.

It had to be Ben, she thought, as she went along the hall. If it wasn't Angie—and she didn't think her mother would make another visit at this time of day—it had to be him. Oh, God, she thought despairingly, this was all she needed.

The bell pealed again as she reached the door, and she knew a moment's indignation. So impatient! she thought, reaching for the handle. He must have seen the car. He knew she was at home. Couldn't he show a little consideration?

At first glance, the woman who was waiting outside was unfamiliar to her. Jaime, preparing herself for a confrontation with Ben, was taken off balance, and the relief she felt was tempered with a weak sense of anti-climax. 'Yes?'

'Don't you recognise me?' The woman, who appeared to be in her late sixties, gave her an arrogant stare, and Jaime felt a disturbing twinge of alarm.

'No, I—I——' She faltered, and the woman's lips curled.

'Oh, I'm sure you will remember me, if you think hard enough,' she declared, looking beyond Jaime to where Tom had come to stand in the kitchen doorway. 'He knows who I am, don't you, Tom?'

And then Jaime knew, too. But her hesitation had been understandable enough. It was more than fifteen years since that memorable occasion Philip had taken her to meet his parents, and Mrs Russell's face was not one she had wanted to remember.

'It's Mrs Russell, Mum,' Tom said behind her, as Jaime demanded tautly,

'What do you want?'

'A few words is all,' replied Mrs Russell, with equal hostility. 'May I come in?'

'I don't think so.' Jaime glanced over her shoulder at Tom, wishing he would just go back into the kitchen and close the door. 'We have nothing to say to one another.'

'I disagree.'

Mrs Russell put one foot on the threshold, and Jaime gazed at it in amazement. What did Ben's mother hope to do? Force her way inside? She might be a tall woman—like her sons—and strong for her age, but surely she couldn't hope to compete with a much younger adversary.

Deciding it would be too embarrassing for all concerned to try to find out, Jaime tried to ignore it. 'Well, I'm sorry,' she said, 'but I don't care what you think. Now, if you don't mind——'

'You'd prefer me to say what I have to say here?' Mrs Russell waved a dismissing hand, and, as she did so, Jaime noticed Curtis leaning on the bonnet of the Mercedes, which was parked in the road, outside her gate. So his mother had Ben's blessing, did she? Jaime thought tremulously. Was this his way of getting back at her? By letting his mother fight his battles for him?

'I don't particularly care what you have to say,' she said at last, casting another speaking look in Tom's direction, but instead of taking the hint, and returning to his dinner, the boy came forward.

'Why don't you go away, as Mum says?' he asked, and Jaime gave an inward groan as Mrs Russell turned her scornful gaze on him.

'I suggest you speak when you're spoken to,' she retorted. 'And the sooner you're transferred to a school where they'll teach you to show some respect for your elders the better.'

'Transferred to another school?'

Tom was shocked, and showed it, and Jaime briefly closed her eyes against the damage this woman could unknowingly inflict. 'Look,' she said, stepping in front of her son, and pressing him back along the hall, 'I don't know why you've come here, and I don't want to know. You—you've hurt Tom enough, and I won't allow you to do this. I want you to go——'

'How typical!' Mrs Russell sneered. 'You accuse me of hurting Tom, when all these years you're the one who's hurt him most!'

'That's not true——'

'It is true.' Mrs Russell was adamant. 'You're a past mistress at hurting people, Jaime. First Philip, then Tom, and now Ben!'

'Ben?' Jaime's lips twisted. 'I doubt if he'd appreciate your saying that.'

'No?'

'No.' Jaime realised Tom hadn't gone back into the kitchen, as she had hoped, but some things had to be said. 'Ben's pretty good at hurting people himself. What about——' it was a calculated risk '—what about Maura?'

'Oh—Maura!' Mrs Russell swept her late daughter-in-law aside with a careless hand. 'Maura doesn't come into this. Besides, she's been dead for more than three years. Very sad, of course, but Ben should never have married her. As soon as he found out, he should have divorced her. I mean she knew, before the wedding. She should have told him.'

Jaime blinked. 'Knew? Knew what?'

'That she had leukaemia, of course. Didn't Ben tell you? Oh, of course, he wouldn't. What a pity *she* didn't marry Philip.'

Jaime swayed. 'Why?' she whispered, as a kaleido-scope of images swept over her. Ben at her wedding, *without* Maura. Ben rescuing her from Philip, also without Maura. Ben's reluctance to talk about his wife—her reclusiveness. His refusal to leave Maura, even though he had said he loved Jaime. Dear God, was that why he had left England? To remove the chance of ever seeing her again?

'Why?' Mrs Russell was saying. 'I should have thought that was obvious. Then we wouldn't be in this situation, and I might have some legitimate grandchildren!'

Jaime felt sick. 'I think you'd better go——'

'Not before I say what I've come for,' declared the other woman grimly. 'I just thought you ought to know what you've done!'

Jaime swallowed. 'What I've done?' she echoed, and Tom grabbed her arm, and said,

'Don't listen to her, Mum.'

'Yes, what you've done,' continued Mrs Russell, ig-noring Tom completely. 'You've put my son in hospital, that's what you've done! As I say, you know all about hurting people, Jaime. I just hope you haven't killed him, that's all.'

Jaime clutched the door for support, and even Tom pressed forward to hear what was being said. 'In hos-pital?' he got out bravely. 'I—I don't believe you.'

'Ask Curtis, then,' said Mrs Russell contemptuously. 'If you don't believe me, ask him. He'll tell you Ben collapsed after your mother left this morning. He'll tell you how Ben had to be rushed to the hospital in Kingsmere for an emergency operation!'

'Oh, God!' Jaime slumped against the door. 'I—I've got to go to him,' she whispered frantically, but Tom was tugging at her arm.

'*You*—you went to see Uncle Ben this morning?' he exclaimed, and now she could see anger in his face, too. 'Why didn't you tell me?'

'Not now, Tom,' she pleaded, very near to breaking-point, but Tom had his own reasons for distrusting her.

'You weren't going to tell me, were you?' he de-manded, as Mrs Russell looked on with scathing eyes. 'You pretend not to like him, but as soon as anything happens you can't wait to get in touch with him, can you? Why? Are you in love with him or something? Was Uncle Ben the reason you left his brother?'

'No!' Jaime was still desperate to go and see Ben, but she had to disabuse Tom of that belief. 'I left Philip for reasons I couldn't begin to go into at this moment. Suffice it to say, he was a sick man, and he made my life a living hell! Now—I've got to go——'

'But why?' Tom retained his hold on her, and, gazing into his troubled face, Jaime knew she couldn't keep the truth from him any longer.

'Because he's your father!' she cried, and, snatching her arm out of his stunned grasp, she pushed past Mrs Russell, and ran down the path.

CHAPTER THIRTEEN

BEN was in a side-ward. He was still unconscious, but, according to the doctor Jaime had spoken to, he was not in any immediate danger. He had had the operation his mother had spoken of, and was presently recovering from the anaesthetic. He was still attached to a drip, and another machine monitored his heartbeat but, again according to his surgeon, he was expected to make a full recovery.

The relief was so great that Jaime spent the first five minutes after receiving this news being sick. She emptied her stomach of everything she had had that day, and when she managed to return to Ben's room she felt like nothing so much as crawling into bed beside him.

Not that the ward sister would have taken a very favourable view if she had. When Jaime arrived at the hospital, after prevailing upon Curtis to disobey Mrs Russell's commands and bring her, she had had quite a problem trying to convince the starchy sister that she had a legitimate right to be there. Mrs Russell, who had insisted on accompanying them, had done her best to thwart her efforts, and it was not until Ben's doctor appeared and ascertained that this was the 'Jaime' Ben had apparently been asking for before the operation that she was permitted into his room. And it was the doctor who suggested that Mrs Russell should wait in the visitors' lounge until Ben regained consciousness. It wasn't wise for a patient to be over-stimulated, and as *Jaime* was here...

So, by some miracle, it was Jaime alone who was sitting beside Ben's bed when he eventually opened his eyes. She saw the flicker of his lashes, and the languid way his lids lifted, and for a moment she was too over-whelmed to say anything. But then Ben's eyes focused and turned in her direction, and she could no longer contain her relief.

'Oh, Ben,' she breathed unsteadily, getting to her feet and leaning over him. 'Thank God, you're all right.' She lowered her head and bestowed a trembling kiss at the corner of his mouth. 'I—I thought—oh, I don't know what I thought. I—I've been so worried!'

Ben frowned, as a tear dropped from her lashes on to his face. But he put out his tongue to remove it, before saying huskily, 'How did you get here?'

'Oh, it's a long story,' said Jaime, cupping his face in her hands, as if she couldn't get enough of looking at him. 'You've been ill. You wanted me. Do you remember?'

'I've wanted you a long time,' he said, lifting his hand to cover one of hers. 'I'll have to be ill more often, if this is what happens.'

'Oh, Ben.' Jaime kissed him again. 'I love you.'

'Do you?' Ben's eyes darkened. 'I thought you hated me.'

'Oh, no.' Jaime sniffed, in no state to hide her emotions any longer. 'I wanted to. I did. But you knew it wasn't true.'

'Did I?'

'You should. After—after what happened this morning.'

'What happened this morning?'

'You know.' Jaime's lips were tremulous. 'You must.'

'Refresh my memory,' he said, and the faint smile that touched the corners of his lips convinced her that he really was going to be all right.

'No,' she said. 'Not now. Now, I've got to tell your mother that you're OK. She—she's in the waiting-room.'

'My mother?' Ben blinked. 'What's she doing here?'

'The same as me,' said Jaime soothingly. 'Making sure you're all right. I expect Curtis sent for her when you were taken ill. I don't know. Anyway, it's thanks to her that I'm here. Well, not thanks to her exactly, but she did tell me what had happened——'

'She told you I had had an operation, did she?'

'In a manner of speaking——'

'Did she tell you what it was for?'

Jaime shrugged. 'No. But that doesn't matter. As long as you're going to be all right.'

'It does matter.' Ben sighed. 'Jaime, it was only a perforated appendix——'

'Only!' Jaime's heart fluttered.

'Well, it was nothing—life-threatening. I mean, they caught it in time,' said Ben wearily. 'I'm sorry if you——'

'If I what?'

'Oh——' Ben groaned '—if you thought I was dying, or something. I admit, I did have a viral infection when I came back from Africa, and that complicated matters, but I know what my mother's like. I know how vindictive she can be, and if she thought that you—that you and I—Jaime, I don't want there to be any lies between us ever again.'

'There won't be. I promise.' Jaime inched her way on to the side of the bed, and smoothed the damp hair back from his forehead. 'All right, maybe I would have taken a little longer to come to my senses if she hadn't put the fear of God into me. But she also—told me something else. About—about Maura. Ben, why didn't you tell me she had leukaemia?'

Ben looked puzzled. 'But you knew!'

'No, I didn't.'

'Philip must have told you?'

'No.'

'Oh, God!' Ben captured one of her hands in both of his. 'You mean—you mean you didn't know why I couldn't leave her?'

'No.'

'God!' He raised her fingers to his lips. 'But I thought everyone knew. Everyone in the family, that is.'

'But I wasn't really part of the family, was I?' Jaime reminded him gently. 'Your mother saw to that.'

'So she did.' Ben shook his head. 'Do you mean—you might have told me about Tom if—if——?'

'I don't know.' Jaime bent her head. 'You went off to Africa——'

'Because I couldn't bear the thought that there was some other man in your life,' said Ben harshly. 'Don't you remember? You told everyone you were going away with—with another man?'

'Oh, Ben.' Jaime lowered her head to rest her chin on their clasped hands. 'And I thought that you—that you——'

'Didn't care?' he demanded huskily. 'If you only knew!'

'Well, I do now,' said Jaime unsteadily. 'From now on, there won't be any more mistakes. The only people who matter are you, and me, and Tom—oh, God! *Tom!*'

'What is it?' Ben gazed at her anxiously. 'There's nothing wrong with Tom, is there?'

'I told him,' confessed Jaime weakly. 'I've just remembered. I told him about you. That you're his father. Oh, God, I was in such a state, it just came out. What must he be thinking?'

Ben made a helpless gesture. 'He had to know,' he said. 'Sooner or later, he was bound to learn the truth. Particularly in the present circumstances.' His hands tightened around hers. 'OK, maybe he didn't find out in the kindest way possible, but he's my son as well as yours. He'll get over it. With our help.'

'*Our* help,' said Jaime unsteadily. 'Oh, that sounds good to me.'

'And to me,' said Ben, drawing a laboured breath. 'Oh, God, Jaime, do you have any idea how much I need you?'

'What you need is a little bit of rest and relaxation, Mr Russell,' declared the ward sister's reproving voice from the doorway. 'And you won't get it if members of your immediate family insist on disrupting your convalescence. Hey, young man! Where do you think you're going? I haven't given you permission to go in there yet——'

But it was too late. As Jaime got reluctantly to her feet, Tom pushed past the nurse, and came uncertainly to his father's bedside. He didn't look at his mother. His whole attention was centred on the man in the narrow hospital bed, and Jaime watched, dry-mouthed, as he halted at the foot of it.

There was a moment's silence, when even the nurse seemed aware of the tension in the room, and then Ben said softly, 'Hi, Tom!' and Tom's unnatural composure cracked.

'Hi—Ben,' he replied, moving a little nearer. 'How—how are you?'

'Improving by the minute,' said Ben, with some relief, exchanging a tense look with Jaime. 'How about you?'

'Me?' Tom did look at his mother now, but even she could read nothing from his expression. 'I'm not the one who's in hospital. Sister Latimer says you're as well as can be expected.'

Ben looked at the disapproving face of Sister Latimer, and reserved comment. 'I'm OK,' he said, and, as if her patience was at last exhausted, Sister Latimer marched across the floor.

'I'm sorry, Mrs Russell,' she said. 'But your husband must get some rest.'

'He's not my——' began Jaime, and then, catching Ben's eyes, she closed her mouth. 'Oh—all right.' She squeezed the hand she was still holding. 'But I'll come back later, if I may?'

'Tomorrow,' declared Sister Latimer firmly, and even though Jaime protested she was unyielding. 'It's late, Mrs Russell. And our patient needs to get some sleep. Now, if you don't mind...'

Jaime sighed, but it was obvious that the sister only had Ben's interests at heart. 'Very well,' she said, releasing his reluctant fingers. 'Um—say goodbye, Tom.'

Tom hesitated. Then, risking the nurse's displeasure, he thrust his hands into his pockets, and said, 'Is it true? What—what Mum said?'

'Mrs Russell——' began the sister impatiently, but Ben had reached out a hand, and after a few seconds Tom took it.

'I'm afraid so,' he said, giving his son a rueful grimace. 'We'll talk about it tomorrow. And don't—don't blame your mother. It wasn't her fault.'

An hour later, Jaime and Tom were seated, side by side, on a rather lumpy sofa in the visitors' lounge. In spite of her forbidding appearance, Sister Latimer had agreed that both Jaime and her son could stay the night at the hospital, just in case there were any unforeseen difficulties. Not that she expected there would be, she maintained, after showing them the side-ward with its two narrow beds, where they were expected to sleep. But she seemed to understand their reluctance to leave, and had even provided the tray of tea and sandwiches that stood on the table beside them.

Mrs Russell, Senior, had departed some time ago, complaining bitterly that she should be the one to stay at her son's bedside. But happily Sister Latimer's word was final, and, after allowing Mrs Russell a brief word with her son, she had advised her to come back in the morning.

So now only Jaime and Tom remained in the waiting-room, each of them, in their own way, suffering the after-effects of what had happened. Jaime felt both scared and elated, but the fact that Tom hadn't spoken an unsolicited word to her since he arrived at the hospital was rapidly draining her resources.

'Would you like some more tea?' she asked. Although they hadn't touched the sandwiches, they had both welcomed a hot drink, and now Jaime indicated the teapot with an inviting hand. But Tom only shook his head, and once again they lapsed into the uneasy silence that had reigned before she spoke.

Jaime sighed and, resting her elbows on her knees, she cupped her chin in her hands. As hospital waiting-rooms went, it was not unattractive, she thought, trying to distract herself. Cream walls, cream paintwork, and chocolate-brown carpet and drapes. Even the sofas were colour-co-ordinated, even if their springing left something to be desired.

'Why didn't you tell me?'

The question she had been waiting for, ever since she'd blurted out the truth about Tom's parentage, came as little more than a whisper, and Jaime's heart turned over.

'I couldn't,' she said, looking at her son with helpless eyes. 'I wanted to, but I couldn't.'

'Why not?'

'It's a long story.'

'We've got plenty of time.'

'Yes.' Jaime had to concede that they had. All night, in fact. And Tom deserved the whole story. 'Well—where shall I begin?'

'How about—at the beginning?' suggested Tom tensely. 'Were you expecting me when you married Philip?'

'No!' Jaime was horrified. 'Why would you think that?'

'Well, you did tell me my dad—my dad was a married man, didn't you? And—and Uncle—I mean Ben—was married, wasn't he?'

'Oh, I see.' Jaime expelled her breath weakly. 'But no. It was nothing like that. I didn't even know Ben when I married Philip. The first time I met him was at the wedding.'

Tom nodded. 'Go on.'

Jaime sighed. It wasn't going to be easy. Tom was still such a child in some ways, and what she had to tell him wasn't pretty. But it was necessary, she acknowledged, and with grim determination she outlined the stark details of her life with Philip Russell.

Tom broke in once, to clarify exactly how Philip had threatened her parents, but after that he remained silent. It was obvious that he was disgusted by the way she had been treated, and Jaime blamed herself for having to violate his innocence.

'But how did Uncle—I mean, how did—my father—persuade Philip to stay away from you?' he asked, some time later, and Jaime hunched her shoulders.

'He—took me to see a doctor, and they took—pictures,' she explained unwillingly. 'And Philip knew Ben wouldn't hesitate to use them. If he had to.'

Tom shook his head. 'And that was when you and—and——'

'Ben got together?' suggested Jaime wryly. 'No. Not for another year. Oh, I'm not denying he didn't come to see me. He did. He sort of acted as a go-between, between me and Philip. And—we became friends. More than friends. Eventually.'

Tom chewed on his lip. 'Did he—did he love you?'

'I thought he did.'

'But he was married, right?'

Jaime nodded. 'Right.'

'Then he was to blame——'

'Not exactly.' Jaime clasped her hands together. 'I—I was the one who—wanted to change our relationship. I thought Ben would leave his wife if he loved me. But—he couldn't.' She grimaced. 'Only I didn't know that then.'

'What do you mean?'

'Well——' Jaime's nails dug into her palms '—after—after we had become—lovers—I didn't see Ben for weeks. I suppose he was avoiding me, but I didn't know why. Then he came and told me that—that he wasn't going to see me again. That our relationship was over. That he had no intention of leaving Maura. His wife.'

Tom's eyes darkened. 'So he did abandon us!'

'Not *us*, Tom. Me! He didn't know about you. Not until—not until that night he came to our house. The night I was at the Haines's party.'

'But why didn't you tell him? Why didn't you *make* him leave his wife?'

Jaime shook her head. 'I couldn't do that. I was sure he didn't love me, you see. I thought he had just wanted an affair. How could I tell him I was pregnant? I had some pride left, in spite of everything.'

'Oh, Mum!'

'Let me finish.' Jaime covered the hand he had placed on her arm, and offered him a rueful smile. 'Where was I? Oh, yes. I was pregnant, and not yet divorced from Philip. I had to go away. I was afraid, even then, that Philip might find out, and claim the child was his. So I went to your grandfather's sister in Newcastle, and you were born there.'

'So—there was no *other* man?'

'No.'

'Just—just—Ben?'

'Your father. Yes.'

Tom frowned. 'And he went off to Africa, with his wife?'

'His sick wife, yes.'

'His *sick* wife?' Tom frowned. 'You never said she was sick!'

'Because I didn't know. Not until tonight, when—when your other grandmother was so scathing about her.'

'Of course.' Tom remembered. 'She said she had leukaemia.'

'That's right.'

'But didn't—didn't my father tell you?'

'Why would he?' Jaime shrugged. 'He thought I knew. He assumed Philip had told me.'

'So—that was why he stayed—with his wife?' ventured Tom unsteadily, and Jaime nodded. 'And he never knew about me?'

'No.'

'But when he came back——'

'Yes, when he came back, he told me Maura was dead,' agreed Jaime heavily. 'But, as far as I was concerned, the situation hadn't changed. I still didn't trust him, and when he found out about you...'

Tom perked up. 'He wanted to get to know me.'

'Yes.' Jaime squeezed his hand. 'He's very proud of you.'

Tom's face flushed, and his eyes grew unnaturally bright. 'I—I'm proud of him, too.'

Jaime smiled. 'I'm sure you are.'

'But——' Tom faltered '—what about you? How—how do you feel?'

'About Ben?' And at his nod, 'I love him. I suppose I always have. I just—blotted it out for a while.'

Tom hesitated. 'Do you think—do you think you might—forgive him now?'

Jaime's eyes were bright, too. 'I think there's every possibility,' she admitted huskily, and pulled him into her arms.

Three months later, Jaime awakened in the king-size bed that Ben had installed in the master bedroom at the Priory, and lay for a few moments, trying to get her bearings. Two days before, she had awakened in Hawaii, in the bedroom of the beach-house on Maui that Ben had rented for their honeymoon. But now, two nights and about seven thousand miles later, they were home again, and she turned eagerly to her husband, needing to assure herself that it was real, and not just some fantastic dream.

But she didn't really need that reassurance. The languid state of her body, the lingering sense of lethargy she felt from Ben's lovemaking of the night before was proof enough, if proof were needed. For four idyllic weeks she had been Mrs Benjamin Russell, and pretty soon she would have to tell him that he was going to be a father again.

As if sensing his wife was awake, Ben stirred now, and his body curled around hers, his hand on the slight curve of her stomach, propelling her back against him. 'G'morning,' he murmured, rubbing the stubble of his overnight beard against her shoulder. 'Did you sleep well?'

'Eventually,' said Jaime, with a chuckle, arching her rounded bottom closer to his muscled maleness. 'Mm, what time is it? It looks awfully light outside.'

'Don't do that, if you want to talk about the time,' complained Ben, as his body reacted to her nearness. 'Oh, hell, what does it matter? Let's spend the day in bed. We can always say we need to get over the jet lag.'

'Not to Tom,' Jaime reminded him softly. 'How do you think he looked last night? Do you think he's missed us at all?'

Ben chuckled now. 'Well, he does seem to have taken over in our absence,' he agreed drily. 'And he and Curtis get along like a house on fire. But, of course, they always did.'

Jaime wriggled on to her back, and looked at him. 'What about your mother? She seems to have mellowed somewhat, doesn't she?'

'Mm.' Ben bent his head to nuzzle the taut curve of her nipple with his lips, and then, when Jaime protested, he added resignedly, 'Well, he is her only grandchild, isn't he? And she and Dad aren't getting any younger.'

'No.' Jaime was debating whether to tell him her news then, or wait until she had had it confirmed by a doctor, when Ben went on,

'I guess we've all made mistakes. Me more than most. So who am I to make judgements, when my own decisions have been so suspect?'

'You mean, mine were,' declared Jaime, lifting her hand to stroke his cheek. 'I shouldn't have jumped to conclusions. But we do crazy things when we've been hurt.'

'Don't I know it?' Ben moistened her lips with his tongue. 'Like not telling you why I came to see you in the first place. You might not have believed me, but I should have taken that chance.'

Jaime's brows drew together. 'About Philip, you mean?'

'No.' Ben's thumb brushed her parted lips. 'About me. About why I bought this place. It wasn't by accident, you know. I wanted to be near you.'

Jaime stared at him. 'But—but I thought——'

'I know what you thought.' Ben grimaced. 'When you saw me, you came at me like a mad woman. If I hadn't had my suspicions before then, I'd surely have had them later. It was obvious you were running scared, and it didn't take me long to work out why. God, you have no idea how I felt when I realised you'd kept Tom's identity a secret for almost fifteen years!'

Jaime bent her head. 'So you decided to keep Philip's death a secret, too?'

'I had my reasons,' Ben admitted honestly. 'At least it gave me a chance to go on seeing you. Both of you.'

'But why did you wait so long?' Jaime exclaimed. 'You said Maura had been dead for—for several years.'

'She had.' Ben nodded. 'But don't forget I thought you were living with someone else. I knew you had had a child. My mother wrote and told me. No doubt she was hoping it would cast some aspersions on your reputation, and I was too sick at the thought to attempt to prove otherwise. Then, when I got back to England and found out you and Tom were living alone...'

'Oh, Ben!' Jaime slid her arm around his neck and buried her face against his bare chest. 'I'm sorry.'

'Don't be.' Ben lifted her chin and kissed her. 'It's probably just as well you didn't tell me about the baby. I was trying to do the honourable thing. I knew I couldn't abandon Maura, not when she knew she—well, you know. But, if I'd suspected that you were expecting my child——' he broke off with a wry exclamation '—I don't know whether I'd have had the strength to let you go.'

Jaime sniffed. 'Oh, love...'

'I just wish I could have been there for you,' Ben murmured, sliding his fingers into her hair. 'It can't have been easy, and there's so much about Tom I've missed.'

'Like watching him grow up?' suggested Jaime huskily, and when Ben nodded the decision was taken for her. 'So—perhaps you won't mind too much if we have another.'

'Another what? Another child?' Ben cupped her nape. 'Sweetheart, I may be too old to father another child. After all, Maura and I never—well, you know what I'm trying to say.'

Jaime drew back and touched his lips with her fingers. 'I'm trying not to be jealous of Maura. I mean, I've got so much. But did you—did you—love her?'

'Yes.' Ben didn't attempt to lie to her. 'But not as I love you. I didn't even know you could love someone like this until I met you, and then it was too late. Or so I thought, anyway.'

Jaime accepted this. She knew, better than anyone, how much Ben loved her, and she could afford to be generous now. 'So you wouldn't mind if we had another baby,' she whispered softly, drawing his hand down to the gentle swell below her navel. 'Like—soon?'

Ben's expression was incredulous. 'You mean——?'

'Hmm.' Jaime's smile was tremulous. 'In about six months, I think.'

'But, that means——'

'I know. That morning in the library, when I was so afraid someone might come in and see us.' She pulled a face. 'The day you had your operation.'

'God!' Ben pushed himself up on one elbow and looked down at her. 'That's incredible!'

'But—you don't mind?'

'Mind?' Ben's kiss was swift and devastating. 'I'm—oh, God!—I'm delighted. But what about you? I mean, it's fifteen years since you had Tom. Are you sure you want to start again?'

'Quite sure.' Jaime slipped her arms around his neck, and pulled him down to her. 'Besides, I've never believed in only children.'

Ben's hand halted in its sensual slide down her body. 'Tom,' he said. 'How do you think he'll take it?'

'I think he's old enough to understand the facts of life,' murmured Jaime, guiding Ben's hand to the swell of her breast. 'Ask Angie.'

'Yes.' Ben's response was husky. 'I'm not at all sure we should have let him stay on at that school. He is only fifteen, after all.'

'But quite a mature fifteen,' declared Jaime firmly. 'And he's going to make a marvellous baby-sitter, don't you think?'

'Well—big brother anyway,' agreed Ben, becoming distracted. 'As long as he doesn't think about making us grandparents for some time yet...'

HARLEQUIN PRESENTS®

A Year
DOWN UNDER

In 1993, Harlequin Presents celebrates the land down under. In June, let us take you to the Australian Outback, in OUTBACK MAN by Miranda Lee, Harlequin Presents #1562.

Surviving a plane crash in the Australian Outback is surely enough trauma to endure. So why does Adrianna have to be rescued by Bryce McLean, a man so gorgeous that he turns all her cherished beliefs upside-down? But the desert proves to be an intimate and seductive setting and suddenly Adrianna's only realities are the red-hot dust *and* Bryce....

Share the adventure—and the romance— of A Year Down Under!

Available this month in
A YEAR DOWN UNDER

SECRET ADMIRER
by Susan Napier
Harlequin Presents #1554
Wherever Harlequin books are sold.

Harlequin is proud to present our best authors and their best books. Always the best for your reading pleasure!

Throughout 1993, Harlequin will bring you exciting books by some of the top names in contemporary romance!

In June,
look for
*Threats and
Promises* by

The plan was to make her nervous....

Lauren Stevens was so preoccupied with her new looks and her new business that she really didn't notice a pattern to the peculiar "little incidents"—incidents that could eventually take her life. However, she did notice the sudden appearance of the attractive and interesting Matt Kruger who *claimed* to be a close friend of her dead brother....

Find out more in THREATS AND PROMISES... available wherever Harlequin books are sold.

Where do you find hot Texas nights, smooth Texas charm,
and dangerously sexy cowboys?

WHITE LIGHTNING

by Sharon Brondos

Back a winner—Texas style!

Lynn McKinney knows Lightning is a winner and she is
totally committed to his training, despite her feud with her
investors. All she needs is time to prove she's right. But
once business partner Dr. Sam Townsend arrives on the
scene, Lynn realizes time is about to run out!

CRYSTAL CREEK reverberates with the exciting rhythm of
Texas. Each story features the rugged individuals who live
and love in the Lone Star State. And each one ends with
the same invitation...

Y'ALL COME BACK...REAL SOON!

**Don't miss WHITE LIGHTNING by Sharon Brondos.
Available in June wherever Harlequin books are sold.**